Rebels With

REBELS WITHOUT A CLUE?

Why the new socialists are anti-poor, badly read and probably poorly dressed

By Douglas J Shaw

Global Press

Rebels Without a Clue?

Copyright © 2004 Douglas J Shaw

All rights reserved. No part of this book may be reproduced or transmitted in any form or by any means, electronic or mechanical, including photocopying, recording, or by any information storage and retrieval system, without the prior written permission of the Publisher.

Global Press
Johannesburg
South Africa
dougieshaw@bigfoot.com

ISBN 0 9533306 1 3

Printed in South Africa.

Rebels Without a Clue?

BRIEF CONTENTS

Introduction: A PRECISE OF CONVERGING TRENDS

Ch1 THERE ARE NO PROBLEMS GOVERNMENTS CAN SOLVE AS WELL AS MARKETS

Ch2 SOCIALISM AND VALUES

Ch3 HOW MARKETS WORK AND WHY BETTER THAN SOCIALISM

Ch4 WEALTH, POVERTY AND MARKETS

Ch5 WHERE WE ARE AND WHERE WE ARE GOING

Ch6 TAX, GOVERNMENT AND IMPLEMENTATION

Ch7 NON-ECONOMIC/ NON ETHICAL OBJECTIONS ANSWERED FAMILY

Ch8 INTERNATIONAL

Ch9 INSECURITY

Ch10 INDIVIDUAL SITUATIONS AND COUNTRIES

Rebels Without a Clue?

Detailed Contents

Introduction:
A PRECISE OF CONVERGING TRENDS

Ch1 THERE ARE NO PROBLEMS GOVERNMENTS CAN SOLVE AS WELL AS MARKETS

Why using markets works so well
Free Markets Produce more Growth anywhere in the world in every decade
Historically the free market has always been a source of prosperity, socialism never is

Ch2 SOCIALISM AND VALUES

Socialism has kept Africa Poor
Socialism is based on theft and envy
Socialism is based on force
The Free Market is based on service not greed.
Capitalism is not survival of the fittest
Capitalism is not force but voluntary exchange
Capitalism is about giving
The Free Market is about Creativity
Free market is about Freedom
Socialism destroys the family
Sin is not in the system, its in the nature of man
The Free Market works when people are wicked (unlike socialism) but works even better when people are good (unlike socialism)
Utopianism: Should we make the world even more imperfect by ignoring market solutions?
Socialists have killed millions of innocent people
Socialist Atrocities
Socialism and communism are exactly the same thing
Common Misconception: Is It All About Money?
Common Misconception: Is Socialism All About Groups, And Capitalism About Individuals?
Socialism and the Destruction of Human Capital
Alternative elites: businesses with the power to service or political appointees with the power to destroy.
Common Misconception: Is "unbridled" or "cutthroat" competition really something to be avoided?
Should business have a "social conscience"?

Rebels Without a Clue?

Claiming something is "owned by the people" usually means it is been stolen from one of them.
A right to sponge?
Common Misconception: Are people becoming more selfish and less loyal?
Inequality
 Common Misconception: Does most of the money in society go to "greedy" businessmen and investors who are all rich
Why businessmen cannot get away with paying less than the just wage.
Human Welfare more than GDP/capita
Socialism Is Not Simply Wrong It Is A Deception
Killing the Golden Goose: socialism by forced sharing destroys what there is to share
Litter and sexual harassment are symptoms of government ownership
Winner takes all
Problems with democracy
Should it be to everyone according to his need
The Left's strategy is all about elites telling ordinary people what to do
The Importance that no criminal organisations are seen as legitimate

Ch3 HOW MARKETS WORK AND WHY BETTER THAN SOCIALISM
Incentives
Public Choice
Information
Price mechanism
The market is a discovery process
The State Took Over From the Private Sector Everything Is Does. It Never Innovates Or Produces Better Solutions
Free market planning
The division of labour
In A Free Market Ordinary People Are In Control, Under Socialism An Elite Decide For You (Dembovsky)
The Market Needs Property Rights to Work
Common Misconception: That Socialism Can Ever Work Long Term. (Anderson 2002)
The Profit Motive as the Foundation of Economic Improvement
Technical
What about "Market Failure"?
Public Goods
Equilibrium
Measurement Issues
The Inevitability Of The Free Market

Rebels Without a Clue?

CH4 WEALTH, POVERTY AND MARKETS

Socialist ideas cause poverty
Socialism is far more dehumanizing than capitalism
High growth caused by capitalism: the best way to help the poor
Do the poor really not pay much in the way of tax?
Minimizing the need for charity
The poor in the West
It is not a battle between rich and poor, they need each other.
Owners and Non-owners of capital benefit from it
Soaking the rich hurts the poor
Poor and rich are constantly changing groups
Common Misconception: Is Investing In Human Capital Vs. It and Systems the Issue? (Responding Reich 1997)
Common Misconception: Is Inflation Control An Alternative To Helping The Poor? (Responding To Reich 1997)
Common Misconception: Are High Levels Of Executive Pay A Problem If They Are Based On Results?
Common Misconception: Does Capitalism Only Listen To The Rich? (Anderson 2002)
Labour laws: damaging the poor out of compassion for them
Common Misconception: Are people becoming more greedy and less loyal?
Common Misconception: Eroding wages for Workers?
Inequality
The industrial revolution was a hugely anti poverty step
Unemployment
Business as Big Bad Wolf
The Welfare State did not work as expected.
What Marxism said would happen did not happen.

Ch5 WHERE WE ARE AND WHERE WE ARE GOING

Common Misconception: Have we already gone to some radically privatised extreme?
Common Misconception: Should balance be sought Between Capitalism and Socialism?
Common Misconception: Are nation states really not obsolete?
Common Misconception: Do economies now require you to spend more time at work?
Common Misconception: Does capitalism causes more short term investment than socialism?
Common Misconception: Are there different forms of capitalism: European, US, Asian which we can choose from?

Rebels Without a Clue?

Common Misconception: Are the prevalence of crises, crashed and meltdowns a problem with capitalism?
Bubbles burst whether we have capitalist or socialist policies
The (perfectly) Efficient Market hypothesis is overplayed.

Ch6 TAX, GOVERNMENT AND IMPLEMENTATION

Costs Of Tax Collection
The Avoidance Industry
Tax destroys
How taxation reduces new jobs
Common Misconception: "That people would rather pay tax to make things better"
Common Misconception: "Our Department Just Needs More Money"
These policies are good for the government in power.
Tax cuts are good for governments that want to encourage entrepreneurship
Twinning
Austerity Programs and Structural Adjustment
Government action is involved in the process of moving to free markets

Ch7 NON-ECONOMIC/ NON ETHICAL OBJECTIONS ANSWERED
FAMILY
Common Misconception: Do we need government action to make our families better?
Common Misconception: Less than the minimum amount to support a family?
Labour Mobility and communities
Victimless crimes are not victimless
How to strengthen the family
Common Misconception: Do we need socialism to improve our communities?
Common Misconception: Is socialism really good for the environment?
Common Misconception: Do social objectives and the environment go by the board in free markets?
Common Misconception: Is it better to replace shareholder rights with "stakeholder rights"?
Owner Manager vs. Shareholder
Balancing "Economic" objectives against "Social", Environmental or "Distributional" (responding to Turner 2001 45)
Socialism Produces Ugliness: Failing On Artistic As Well As Moral And Economic Grounds
Common Misconception: Does advertising create false needs?
Common Misconception: Does marketing, journalism and communication inevitably mislead?

Rebels Without a Clue?

The Corporate Governance Problem
Savings and Loans
The clash of cultures and military
The Threat of War
Markets and Psyche

Ch8 INTERNATIONAL
Common Misconception: Should we protect First World jobs from Third World competition?
Common Misconception: We may sink relative to other countries because of globalisation"
Common Misconception: Are multinationals really a threat to our freedom?
Common Misconception: Is it wrong to multinationals to pay workers in the Third world local rates
Common Misconception: Will international trade or technology lead to unemployment?
Common Misconception: Is National Competitiveness Theory really wrong?
Common Misconception: Can we really cut ourselves off from the rest of the world without cost?
The Growth of Less Develop Countries is not likely to materially affect the West
Globalisation and services
Globalisation Déjà vu
Capital Controls, the Tobin Tax and accurate pricing
Localisation

Ch9 INSECURITY
We have met the enemy and it is us
False solutions: Government cushions people against insecurity. Reich's solutions.
Security and Options
Common Misconception: is capitalism a casino?
The Switchover to a Value Creating Economy (Reich 2002 72-74)
"People are scared of loosing their jobs due to rapid change"
Increasing security for some reduces the insecurity of the rest

Ch10 INDIVIDUAL SITUATIONS AND COUNTRIES
Europe
Russia
Mexico
Germany
The US
The Asian Crisis
Japan

Rebels Without a Clue?

Acknowledgments

Thanks to Craig Vaughan for doing the bulk of the editing on the book and to the only sane force at Cancun namely Julian Morris and Kendra Okonski who were kind enough to allow me to use their photos on the cover.

Introduction

A Précis of Converging Trends and Opportunities

This book is about the convergence of a number of mega trends affecting our world at the beginning of the 21st century. Trends that have the power to greatly improve our world contrary to the critics and doomsayers.

The first of these is privatisation. The unequivocal evidence is that overall provision of goods and services is better done by businesses competing in a market than by government. This means that very soon for forward-looking governments, and within 20 years for foolish ones, the market will do everything currently done by the state. This would include provision of justice, policing, education at all levels, healthcare, land registry, roads and regulation. All these will be private functions.

In a previous book "Privatisation for Prosperity" I explain these things in depth. Here I will assume a level of understanding of those concepts.[1] While the techniques and solutions in this book would work while these areas remain in government ownership, they would work far better when these entities are private. This book is building on the future position where they are all private. For the purpose of this book, the term "socialist" will be used to mean someone who believes that there is anything that is currently done with taxation and government control that could not be done better by competing businesses within a free market.

Part of the remit of this book is to find solutions to the problems that are put forth by recent writers on globalisation and the market. Part of this task is showing that some of the things they think are problems, are in fact not problems. The other part is highlighting the genuine problems and using the power of markets, derivatives and technology to solve the problems.

---

1 Shaw, Douglas 2002 Privatisation for Prosperity (Johannesburg: Global Press). You can get the book by emailing me at the address below or on the internet at www.dougieshaw.com/dts1.html or in all good bookshops.

Rebels Without a Clue?

The second mega trend affecting us is the rise of the Internet and the culmination of the falls in prices of IT over the last 30 years. This has led to a transformation of world stock markets symbolized by the way the (electronic) Eurex market managed to take huge amounts of business from incumbent financial markets due to the lower costs of transacting on electronic markets rather than those that involve a large number of staff. Similarly, ECNs (Electronic Communication Networks) have revolutionised the buying and selling of shares, reducing commissions in some cases to fractions of a percentage of their pre revolution amounts. The long and the short of this is that markets have become a very cheap and powerful tool on a per transaction basis. This is fuelling the B2B and B2C revolutions. Like any new technology of the past (cars, railways, films, aircraft, etc) most of the multitude of companies that exist at the beginning will not succeed. However, the technology itself will continue to grow and develop.

Thirdly, the growth of derivatives, financial instruments for managing risk, are affecting us all. Since the 1970s the growth of derivatives has been exploding. While many people see a huge danger to the financial system in these products, I'm a little more sanguine, as I will explain. Certainly adjustments need to take place, but futures and options need to be "democratised" in the same way that stocks and shares have been, and in addition applied to more areas. In the future, I believe you will be able to buy options on virtually any product. If you are not sure you want to send your children to a particular school next year you will be able to buy an option to give you the right but not the obligation to do so. If you want certainty that your services will sell over the month of December then you in September can buy the right but not the obligation to sell them. All these ways to manage the risk of your life will be available to you, at the price at which the exchange of risk is valuable to both parties.
Financial instruments that you will be seeing more of in daily life situations include futures, call and put options, swaps. We will also see the creation of new markets. This kind of financial engineering, that has previously been the reserve just of big banks, can reach ordinary people and become part of our ordinary life.

Fourthly, connected to the Internet , is the rise of Yield (or Capacity) Management. This is what allows low cost airlines to charge so little. Easyjet and Ryan Air in the UK, South West in the US and Kalula in South Africa are all examples. What they do of course is offer lower prices for people that book in advance and manage the prices so that if based on past experience they can see that the flight is filling up too quickly they can raise prices and if too slowly, they can lower them. This leads to full planes which mean a lower overall cost per passenger. In a competitive market it is always the consumer that benefits most.
The other area this has been applied has been in Hotel Management, but as with Airlines the concept is still quite basic compared to its potential, where the number of potential areas of application is huge.

Rebels Without a Clue?

I should mention here that I spend a lot of time talking with governments in Africa. There are therefore scattered references through the book as to how it would work in the African context. I believe that the potential of this kind of approach is even more appropriate to the developing world than to the West. This might seem like a strange thing to say given the relatively low level of technology. However I have realised that the Internet is an intermediate technology through the Internet cafes springing up all over the cities. Actually IS accessible to the vast majority of poor people especially when they may use it only once a month or so to do the transactions that create the highest values in their lives (such as selling a house which would otherwise not be sold). Also Africans will use it when it is the cheapest method, which it often is. Sometimes in fact it will be the only method!

This is a concise book. It is a summary of probably 20 or 30 books on the subjects discussed so there is no doubt that many of the answers given in a paragraph merit whole chapters. However, since this would turn one book into several volumes, we would rather give you the core of the idea or solution and refer you to more exhaustive treatments for deeper analysis thereof. More exhaustive treatments on the market that I would particularly recommend would be Rothbard (1970) "Power and Market", Friedman (1979) "Free to Choose" and Hayek's (1944) "The Road to Serfdom". From a more Christian perspective, North's analysis of Marx is very useful (North 1989). Those who simply want the reason or the answer without all the analysis will hopefully find it here in concise form. In essence this is a book for busy people who want the key answer without necessarily wanting to read as many books as I might wish to!

Finally, this is not so much a book purely for academic interest. We would like as a consultancy company, to get involved in building and implementing what we consider to be the global architecture of the future. Therefore, we are looking to form an alliance of technology companies, investment banks, capital providers, and international marketers to governments to put a system like this together and bring the future into the present. If you are one of these companies, or even if you are not you can contact me on dougieshaw@bigfoot.com

The book looks at commonly asked questions, popular fallacies and the general debate between advocates of globalisation and markets as against advocates of socialism in its various manifestations. In doing this I have answered the questions and points posed by the main books written against the free market in the last five years on both sides of the Atlantic. Among the books that I have reviewed, Robert Reich's "The Future of Success" has a lot of interesting information about trends and future watching and so is probably the most interesting. His book is probably less economically illiterate than most of the others. Reich was in the Clinton cabinet so he

Rebels Without a Clue?

knows at least something of the reality of government. Second is Adel Turner, formerly head of the Confederation of British Industry whose book "Just Capital" again contains some interesting analysis but suffers from the common British problem of not being able to really take an idea and run with it. Many of Turner's points would argue for a full free market, and then he will make a reservation and blunt the whole power of his argument for markets with an inclination to "in between ism". "Just Capital" is a silly title however as no free market advocate believes in doing business with just capital and no labour! Turner, then while wrongly arguing against a full free market model, has also got some interesting points and analysis. Frank in "One Market under God" has definitely got the best title. He is using it sarcastically, but I think replacing thinking of ourselves as nations; "One Nation under God" with Markets (where the people really decide) is a good one! In his chronicle of what the US Conservative Right is doing he is very critical in his language but does not actually provide much in the way of arguments against it. After a revelation of something Gilder has said or some trend, one is left thinking "yes, that sounds reasonable, so what?" when one is apparently supposed to be shocked. He objects to government agencies being compared to Soviet ones but he never justifies why they should not be. Economics tells us they work the same way.

One Market Under God is a fairly well told story, if a little negative, but it does not present too many arguments against the market, more really of a sense of shocked-ness that sympathizers can relate to.

Taken together I believe the authors raise the bulk of the economic issues that most people run into in 21st century life. I hope you enjoy my analysis.

Douglas Shaw BSc (Hons) BA (Hist) MLIA (Dip) MCP

2003
Johannesburg Glasgow Frankfurt

Chapter 1

There are no problems government can solve better than markets

The free market is preferable for a number of reasons

- The market produces growth that improves the incomes of the poor. Therefore, socialism, by denying this growth, keeps the poor in poverty.
- The current welfare state actually creates poverty by tying up productive resources and impairing growth.
- Taxing the rich hurts the poor. The only people who benefit are government employees.
- People, who really cannot help themselves, are better served by private foundations set up from privatisation proceeds, than by government welfare.

Effectiveness of Markets

Free markets are far more effective because:

- Private companies have something to gain from serving, while governments do not.
- It is not possible for governments to have the information needed to know what combination of goods each person needs and wants — which only the market supplies
- Unlike politicians, companies listen to you to ascertain what you want to buy and sell. Governments obviously listen a lot less carefully. Markets then, are the real democracy.
- The process of collecting taxes and then spending them wastes a tremendous amount of money. A privatised society will eliminate this. The costs incurred by individuals in the their buying decisions is much less.
- Aside from the tangible benefits, it is more ethical to run a society on free market lines. Free markets are based on hard work, thrift, freedom and

- service to others, while socialism is based on theft, envy, force and waste. Its effects are the erosion of national morals.
- Socialism gives the state far too much power, which can then be abused by corrupt, or even evil, men. In a free market society there could never have been a Mao or a Stalin, because non-socialist societies do not give governments so much power. Even traditionally socialist countries have realised this, which is why so many are embarking on privatisation around the world.
- The free market does not make people selfish, or materialistic. These are traits inherent in individuals despite the economic system.
- Furthermore, the free market does not need to be perfect in its effects. It just needs to be superior to the alternative in order to be the superior system.
- Privatisation has been very successful in practice, as demonstrated by a large number of success stories in the extensive academic literature written about privatisation.

Alternative Elites: Businesses With The Power To Service Or Political Appointees With The Power To Destroy.

People often complain about the wealth of rich entrepreneurs who have made their wealth by providing goods and services to ordinary people and improving their lives. However, we must remember the alternative is that the rich and powerful are political appointees who have not earned their wealth at all, but simply been given what has been taxed from others. It is surely better for people that earn their wealth to have it than for a political elite that have not earned it. Furthermore, under socialism it is inevitable that the worst will get on top of the society because those who do not want to serve others (as one had to in a market) see a perfect opportunity to extend their power without having to be humble. Hayek (1944 100+) discusses this phenomena in more depth and Rand's "Atlas Shrugged" illustrates it well in a fictional context.

Growth

The free market produces dramatically higher amounts of growth than socialism. The result of this is that the income of every individual rises quicker. This is extremely important for poor countries. Countries with a low growth rate like socialist Sweden or Russia, poor countries would never get out of poverty. However, in regions with free market growth rates like Hong Kong (7.5%), poverty has been greatly reduced. At the growth rate for a completely free market, say 12% or more, even the poorest countries in the world, like many of those in Africa south of the Sahara, with a GDP of around $300 per person per annum, would reach living standards equitable to developed countries within a generation. A totally free market will grow approximately 10% quicker per year, than will a completely socialist one as the World Bank's statistics show. (World Bank 1990)

Even socialists admit this fact: "in terms that are strictly and narrowly economic, it is true that the global free market is incredibly productive. Equally in the contest between free market economies and social market systems free markets are often superior in productivity. There is not much doubt that the free market is the most *economically efficient* type of capitalism" (John Gray 1998 82) Furthermore, when the ideas espoused by Gray, Reich, Turner and the rest (i.e. "moderate the free market") are applied most severely we can see clearly what happens. Gray himself points out that in Russia, under the initial "War Communism" period industrial production fell by 75% and productivity by 70%, which "decimated the working class (Gray 1998 137). Socialism is hardly good then for the poor.

Africa and Economic Growth

The World Bank has found that even in Africa, if the tax to GDP ratio was 10% lower, then that country would grow on average by 1.2% more per year (World Bank 1990). This figure is confirmed by a simple statistical analysis of the rest of the world, which gives a world wide rate of 1.105% more growth for 10% less on the taxation to GDP ratio(Shaw 2003). The same research also found that no countries with average tax/expenditure to GDP ratio over 30, ever had average GDP growth over 4.5% per year. Countries where the ratio was under 20 never had average growth of less than 2%. Barrow also finds a relation between lower government consumption and economic growth (Barro 1997 38-39). Another World Bank study found that the relationship between small governments and high growth is even significant at the 1% level (5% is usually considered significant, 1% is a very strong relationship) (World Bank 1997 170)

Turner's stats, which do not support this conclusion, suffer from what is known in statistics as a "problem of range". Focusing only on developed countries (Turner 2001 261-2), he does not include enough countries with low tax to GDP ratios to show up the results so they are invalid. Because the countries are very close in their policies (quite socialist) we cannot really see the effect of greatly lower tax regimes like Singapore (14% government spending to GDP) and Hong Kong (8%) Even Turner's statistics however might show more of a relationship between tax levels and GDP if they also controlled for other factors such as regulation levels (a reason why Switzerland probably did badly.) High levels of regulation lead to lower growth. Borrowing levels and inflation might also be worth adding. Running the analysis to 2000 would also greatly lift the US stats, which is why it is probably he only did it to 1995! I suspect there might be an even bigger flaw in his analysis however. The public expenditure to GDP looks like it is the current rate not the average over the

Rebels Without a Clue?

time period, which would completely invalidate the results. The current rate might have come down or up rapidly in the last few years, which means that it doesn't give a indication of how these policies affected GDP historically. To be meaningful we need to look at how tax to GDP rates have been over the whole period.

Turner believes Asian countries are only doing well because the growth is "catch up" growth but he recognizes elsewhere that countries with more socialist polices do not get this growth. Any country that is not the leader can benefit from implementing these catch up policies. Therefore, even if we accept his thesis that the growth that comes from free markets only applies to countries that are catching up, the policy conclusions for the developing world are clearly to implement free market policies - deregulate, privatise and thus cut taxes. Even the leader could probably use them to achieve catch up with the second or third countries that might lead in some sectors. The low growth of Switzerland and the US up to 1995 despite lower tax to GDP could be due to being so far ahead to start with. Of those not far ahead, we do see a correlation between free market policies and growth. Of these, the only countries in the sample that excel are Ireland, which dramatically cut its corporation tax rate turning it into Europe's only dragon economy, and Japan which had a low tax/GDP up to 1990.

Catch Up Growth

Turner argues Europe's previous rates of higher growth than the US were catch up rates rather than because of a better system. (Turner 2001 142)
Catch up growth theories while true up to a point, can no longer account for the continuing high growth of free market (i.e. low tax to GDP) tigers in the East. Hong Kong and Singapore continue to grow through their more free market structures, despite having now "caught up" and indeed overtaken the West in GDP/capita. Additionally, without the free market policies, even catch up growth cannot occur. Africa is experiencing growth now that it has adopted free market policies, no catch up growth was really occurring beforehand.

Moreover, how could it be that lower taxes and more privatisation would not create more growth? We know private companies innovate and add value more than governments departments. Having then, everything in the private sector could not avoid producing more growth. It is inevitable.

For further discussion see Friedman (1989 54+) on the superiority of the free market to more centrally planned approaches a la Turner.

We can see these economic phenomena all over the world and throughout history including Russia, China, Hong Kong, Latin America, the US and Japan.

Rebels Without a Clue?

Russia and Economic Growth

At the end of WWII, Russia had the second largest economy in the world. Now it has difficulty feeding its people. Its total output is now less than Italy's or the UK's and the average annual income in Russia is only £1,780, which is a sixth of the British average. Russia may have seemed to have growth mid century but it is intrinsic to socialism that there is no way of measuring the value of output without a market so they can only guess production levels. When the free market was introduced, their GDP stats collapsed, as what they were producing was now effectively valued. This wasn't so much because they were producing things that people wanted and then stopped doing so. What this showed, in effect, was that the growth they thought they had got wasn't real. The growth rate was in effect much lower than they had guessed.

As we have seen, countries with socialist policies always have lower growth than those with out. This obviously affects the welfare of their poorest people. During the 1970s, Peru had an equitable GDP to Chile. Under the rule of the then president, Alan Garcia, Peru taxed and regulated everything. These reforms led to a fall in tax revenues and when the government raised rates, tax yields fell further. This phenomenon is an example of the Laffer curve, where dropping rates can cause increased tax yields and raising them causes less revenue to be collected (Barro, 1997, 38-39).

Neighbouring Chile, however, had more free market policies and by 1990, Chile's per capita GDP was more than double that of Chile's (Barro, 1997, 38). More recently, the new Peruvian government has adapted better policies. While Chile and Peru are in a similar geographical location, an even more compelling argument is that of Haiti and the Dominican Republic, which occupy respective halves of the same island. In 1988, the Dominican Republic, with its more free market economy, had a per capita GDP of $1,509 as opposed to the $319 per capita GDP Haiti (Kennedy 1993, 203,). It seems difficult to believe that

China and Economic Growth

China, realising the inherent errors of socialism, has adopted a more capitalistic approach. Conditions within this country serve as a good illustration of the difference between the systems. The state firms still grow at 3% per year, the collectives at 9.1% while the private companies are currently growing at 57.7% per year (Kennedy 1993, 203,).

Rebels Without a Clue?

Growth in the USA

The USA was not always a paragon of capitalism. During the 1950s, it was the slowest growing of the main industrial economies. In 1960, it cut its tax rates from 90% to dramatically lower rates and as a result – the economy boomed. From this we can see that the high growth/low tax pattern is not a regional anomaly. Any country can experience this if it adopts the appropriate policies. Even if we take the recent bubble out of the equation, the US has grown faster than Europe over the last 15 years thanks to its more market-oriented policies. Despite this, let us not forget the US also has a long way to go before it is fully privatised and deregulated.

Asia and Economic growth

Japan experienced its most rapid growth in the 30 years between 1960 and 1990, owing to its adoption of free market policies. Tax revenues, both in absolute terms, and as a share of world taxes, grew faster than in any other major nation as it cut taxes each year. Government revenue was the lowest as a share of GDP compared to other nations. Low taxes and constant cuts were the key to Japan's industrial success, not its industrial policies which contrary to popular belief, failed in most cases.

Japan's current no growth state resulting from its failure to cut taxes and deregulate, is lauded by Gray (1998 175) who promotes the idea that there can be progress without economic growth. This is insane as economic growth, whether it expresses more waterfalls or medieval castles bought by groups of people for their preservation, more old folks homes staffed or more education places expanded, is hugely necessary to the improvement of the human race in whatever way we might name. Gray's refusal to accept this should make one wary.

Hong Kong is one of the most free market areas in the world. "It does not have import or export duties, or restrictions on investments coming in, or limits on profits going out. There's no capital gains tax, no interest tax, no sales tax, and no tax breaks for [inefficient] companies that cannot make it on their own"

The corporate tax in Hong Kong is 16.5% of profits. The individual tax rate is 15% of gross income. The Hong Kong government runs a permanent budget surplus and consumes only 6.9% of GDP. Hong Kong has no minimum wage, no unemployment benefits, no union boosting legislation, no social security, no national health program, and minimal welfare. Only 1.2% of GDP goes on transfers to the helplessly poor or subsidies to the hopelessly profitless. The unemployment rate is below 3%. Life expectancy in Hong Kong is about 79 years, compared with 76 years in the USA. The infant mortality rate is comparable to that of Britain.

Rebels Without a Clue?

Economic growth in Hong Kong has averaged 7.5% per year for the past twenty years, causing GDP to quadruple since 1975. With barely one tenth of 1% of the world's population, Hong Kong is the world's eighth largest international trader and tenth largest exporter of services. Hong Kong's per capita GDP is $26, 000. Average individual wealth is greater than that of Japan or Germany and it is $5,600 greater than that of Britain. Hong Kong even has an effective police force — with a crime rate lower than that of Tokyo.

Significantly, in the period 1961 to 1971, the number of households in extreme poverty shrank from more than 50% to 16%. This was the era in which the (wise) government did virtually nothing. African and other governments must learn to be as wise.

Gray (1998: 108) argues that the Asian dragons and the US in the 19th century were not fully free market because the governments did intervene. He does not attempt to prove they intervened more than their competitors however, so his case is unproven. What is not in doubt, however, is that however much they intervened in markets, their tax and government spending ratios to GDP were much lower than other countries that did not do as well. This must be our key measure of how "free market" a country is and what makes it grow the fastest. In other words what percentage of the total activities of the country are done by the free market and what percentage is provided by governments.
If these countries had adopted freer markets and even lower tax to GDP then they would have had even higher growth and brought people out of poverty even quicker, as the statistics that be examined above demonstrate.

Gray implicitly admits this a little later. He says, "The restructuring of American industry has enabled it to reclaim markets once thought forever lost to Japan…freeing up markets has engineered a spectacular economic boom." He fails to see at this point that as well as the once off benefit of adjustment, a free market enjoys permanently higher growth rates (Gray 1998 110).

Learning From History

During the sixteenth and seventeenth centuries, the Netherlands had "next to no government" and "no expensive pretensions to greatness" — instead they grew faster than any other country and invented, for example, the wind powered sawmill. The Dutch had free trade while other countries had trade barriers and as a result there were two Dutch masts in the Thames for every British one. By 1780, Britain was the minimal state — no such situation had existed anywhere before or since. There was

Rebels Without a Clue?

no professional police, a tiny army, a country governed by unpaid magistrates meeting four times a year. This was the secret of Britain's greatness!

Gray(1998: 12) argues that contrary to Hayek, that the market was not a naturally occurring phenomena, but a creation of the state in that the British parliament was the first to realize that this was the best way to do things. Does this matter? The point is that it worked! It delivered the goods, unlike the policies that Gray harks back to. The argument is not between artificial versus natural, but between failed socialism and the free market which delivers the goods.

The idea that the market in the 19th century, was on average "Humanly costly" (Gray 1998: 12) compared to other countries is a myth. The income of the British working class rose by four times in the 19th century. Those countries that did not participate, stuck as they were in their socialist policies, did not enjoy this growth. It appears that he has completed missed the point that through the "market experiment" Britain started the industrial revolution and became the richest country in the world with inequality narrowing in the second half of the century.

The reason that Europe emerged as the greatest world power was precisely because the political power was so fragmented, the state was not able to stop economic growth to the same degree as in rival civilizations like China, India, Russia and the Ottoman Empire. The relatively free market in Europe produced prosperity while Statism in other empires destroyed prosperity.

Governments can never improve conditions without making them worse somewhere else. Whenever they pay money out, they are taking away money from somewhere else. It is impossible for this process to produce a wealthy society. Throughout history, it is only when state control has been minimal, that prosperity has increased.

This century, business has increased the capacity to produce wealth by approximately 20 times in developed countries. About a third of this extra capacity has gone on increased material goods production, and half has been used to cut the number of hours worked - for increasing pay. In the USA, the number of hours worked per week has fallen from 66 in 1900 to 36 now. Much of the remainder is spent on healthcare. During the last 50 years, 8-11% of GDP has been allocated to healthcare, as opposed to only 1% of GDP before this. This is the result of the free market meeting human needs. The human cost of the absence of free markets is far higher than in their presence.

It has been argued that there has been a great increase in inequality since more freedom has been introduced in the UK and the USA during the 1980s and 1990s. Actually, for most of this century not only have the poor been getting richer, but their share of the total (growing) pie has increased. In 1954 in Britain, the top 10% of the

Rebels Without a Clue?

population owned 79% of the wealth. In 1971 they owned 65% and by 1985 only 54% of the wealth. While showing that the rich over the long term have not been getting richer like socialists teach, these statistics are really fairly immaterial. What is important is that the actual amount of income that the bottom 10% is earning is rising much faster, as it does under the free market system, than it would have done under socialism. In other words, it is better to have your income double in ten years (as in the Hong Kong scenario), than to have your share of the pie grow from 5% to 6% while the pie stays the same size. What matters to the poor is economic growth (growth of the pie), not distributions of income (share of the pie).

A free market economy allows everyone in a country to more quickly enjoy what only the rich once enjoyed. Goods are produced and distributed more efficiently and everybody's income grows. In terms of the fluctuations of the free market, the rich lose more than the poor do from the free market economy. The poor benefit from the volatility of the free market as they have everything to gain and little to lose from rapid changes.

Chapter 2
Socialism and Values

Socialism is based on theft and envy

The free market is the only ethical economic system. Socialism is based on theft and envy. Socialists are willing to see the incomes of the poor eroded by low rates of growth, as long as money is taken from the rich in the long disproved hope that this process actually helps the poor. Meanwhile, it is alleged that the tenth largest fortune in the world is that of Fidel Castro — all of it stolen from the people with strong-arm tactics, rather than earned in productive labour. That's what happens in practice when we adopt socialism.

The free market rewards those who are hard working, thrifty, and honest and who have faith in the future. It penalises those who are lazy, spendthrift and dishonest. It is in other words, the more ethical of the two systems.

Socialism is based on Force

There are ethical questions about the use of force. The free market system encourages people to make voluntary decisions. The free market is all about freedom. Under socialism people are forced to pay taxes in order to pay for things they may or may not want and this is somehow tolerated in every country in the world. History has shown those who disobeyed the law in many socialist states, were summarily jailed or murdered. Government ownership of anything in society (education, health, policing, and justice) is all about force. Privatised versions would be all about serving us as consumers.

Socialism destroys the family

Socialist countries result in undesirable erosions of morality: In Sweden, the jewel in the socialist crown, divorce is 60% higher than in the US (Gregorsky, 1998: 228) and illegitimacy is three times as high (33% born out of wedlock). The atrocities of Stalin, Mao and the National Socialists (Nazis) are of a horrific scale. It is as clear in practice as in theory that socialism is far from being a moral system. Its pretension to legitimacy comes from its alleged concern for the poor, but as we will see, socialism does not help the poor as well as capitalism does.

Socialists have kept Africa poor.

Socialists should feel some sense of guilt for keeping the world, and particularly Africa, in poverty. Poor countries have used socialist policies that have led to zero income growth compared to the free market rates of 8% or more per year experienced in the Far East. Africa could be where the Asian Dragons are now, were it not for Socialism. The problems that Africa currently faces as a result of these policies are a major reason why no poor country should ever be induced to follow socialist policies.

The Free market is based on Service not Greed

Contrary to Marxist rhetoric, the free market is not based on greed but on service to others. Corrupt socialist bureaucrats can be as motivated by money to the same degree that a businessman can. The gains from their corruption do not benefit society in the same way that the gains from businesses do. Those who prosper in the free market can only legally do so by serving people: by providing the goods and services that consumers want. Under socialism there is no need for people to serve one another, and so they do not. If people become rich in a free market environment they deserve their gains because they have produced goods and services for people — goods and services which, were they not produced by that business, the people would perhaps not be able to buy at the same price or quality either elsewhere or at all.

Franks (2002: 130) as a socialist, cannot stand to see evidence that in general (though obviously not in every single case) it is people with character that grow richer. "The Millionaire Next Door" shows that the average US millionaire is "humble, thrifty and wise" and not the wicked guy that clambers over everyone else to get to the top. This kind of research reduces the credibility of the likes of Franks to take their possessions from them. He is right to say that saving is not a value in itself (it must be spent at some point). However, in a culture where everyone seems to be up to their eyes in debt, it might be good for people to copy the pattern of the "Millionaire Next Door"

Gilder puts it well: "Entrepreneurs work harder than anyone else, in general, and they have to learn more so they also study harder. Entrepreneurs have to raise money and build teams, so they have to co-operate and then they have to respond to the needs of other people" (Gregorsky, 1998: 114). He admits that there may be a few

Rebels Without a Clue?

nasty people running companies but they have succeeded despite, not because, of their negative traits. And again "Lots of people do not *like* to serve others. They think it is below them to serve others. They regard their own self expression as prime value....capitalism accepts the judgment of others [unlike bureaucratic plans or modern art, imposed by an elite even when not demanded]" (Gregorsky, 1998: 128.) In other words, as well as being people & service orientated - unlike government, the market is also humble, receptive to the opinions of others.

The Free Market is not survival of the fittest

Survival of the fittest is not a good analogy with capitalism. Unlike in biology (and there are doubts now that the principle even applies there), everybody gains from each person rising to the level of his ability though competition. Survival of the fittest is a zero-sum game environment - when one person gains another one loses. In free market trade, when one person gains, they do so by producing a gain for someone else. Empirically the case for the evil and rapacious capitalist has a long way to go. According to George Reisman (2002):

> "As von Mises has shown, the economic competition that takes place under capitalism is radically different than the biological competition that prevails in the animal kingdom. In fact, its character is diametrically *opposite*. The animal species are confronted with scarce, nature-given means of subsistence, whose supply they are unable to increase. Man, by virtue of his possession of reason, can increase the supply of everything on which his survival and well-being depend. Thus, instead of the biological competition of animals striving to grab off limited supplies of nature-given necessities, with the strong succeeding and the weak perishing, economic competition under capitalism is a competition in who can increase the supply of things the most, with the outcome being practically everyone surviving longer and better.
>
> The competition of farmers and farm-equipment manufacturers enables the hungry and weak to eat and grow strong; that of pharmaceutical manufacturers enables the sick to recover their health; that of eye-glass and hearing-aid manufacturers enables many who otherwise could not see or hear, to do so. Therefore, far from being a competition whose outcome is "the survival of the fittest," the competition of capitalism is more accurately described as a competition whose outcome is the survival of all or at least of more and more, for longer and longer and ever better. The only sense in which only the "fittest" survive is that it is the fittest *products* and fittest *methods of*

production that survive, until replaced by still fitter products and methods of production, with the effects on human survival just described.

As von Mises has also shown, with his development of Ricardo's law of comparative advantage into the law of association, there is *room for all* in the competition of capitalism. Even those who are less capable than others in every respect have a place. In fact, in large measure, competition under capitalism, so far from being a matter of conflict among human beings, is a process of organising that one great *system of social cooperation* known as the division of labour. It decides at what point in this all-embracing system of social cooperation each individual will make his specific contribution—who, for example, and for how long, will be a captain of industry, and who will be a janitor, and who will fill all the positions in between. In this competition, each individual, however limited his abilities, is enabled to out-compete all others, however superior to him their abilities may be, for his special place. Quite literally, and as an everyday occurrence, those with abilities no greater than required to be a janitor are able to out compete, hands down, without question, the world's greatest productive geniuses—*for the job of janitor.*
For example, Bill Gates might be so superior an individual that in addition to being able to revolutionize the software industry, he might be able to clean five times as many square feet of office space in the same time as any janitor now living, and do it better. However, if Gates can earn a million dollars an hour running Microsoft, and janitors can be found willing to work for, say, $10 an hour, their readiness to perform the job at one one-hundred thousandth of the hourly rate Gates would require, so far dwarfs their lesser abilities that it is they who are "hors de concourse" in this case.

The losses associated with competition are at most short-run losses only. For example, once the blacksmiths and horse breeders put out of business by the automobile found other lines of work on a comparable level, the only lasting effect of the automobile on them was that they too, in their capacity as consumers, came to enjoy the advantages of the automobile over the horse. Similarly, farmers using mules, who were driven out of business by the competition of farmers using tractors, did not die of starvation, but simply had to change their line of work. When they did so, they along with everyone else enjoyed both a more abundant supply of food and of other products as well, which other products could be produced precisely on the foundation of labour released from agriculture.

Even in those cases in which an isolated competition results in an individual having to spend the remainder of his life at a lower station than he enjoyed before, for example, the owner of a buggy-whip factory having to live for the rest of his life as an ordinary wage earner after being put out of business by the automobile—even he cannot reasonably claim that competition has harmed him. The most he can reasonably claim is merely that from this point on, the immense gains he derives from competition are less than the still more immense gains he derived from it previously. For competition is what underlies the production and supply of everything he continues to be able to buy and is what is responsible for the purchasing power of every dollar of his and everyone else's income. And, of course, it proceeds to raise his real income from the level to which it was set back. Indeed, under capitalism, competition proceeds to raise the standard of living of the average wage earner above that of even the very wealthiest people in the world a few generations earlier. (Today, for example, the average wage earner in a capitalist country has a standard of living higher than that even of Queen Victoria, in probably every respect except the ability to employ servants.)" (Reisman 2002)

In voluntary exchange, everybody gains.

An increase in wealth for an individual almost always results in a much greater increase for the world in general. Whenever there is a transaction everybody gains. When you buy a pair of shoes, it is because the shoes are worth more to you than the money spent and the money is worth more to the shop than the shoes. Everybody gains. The entrepreneur who created the project is only able to take a proportion of the shop's gain — the rest goes towards jobs for everyone else. Therefore, the gain to his customers is many times the gain he receives. We can hardly begrudge him such a small percentage of the gain he has created for others.

The Free Market is about Giving

Capitalism starts with giving — it is not primarily based on greed or self-interest, but with regard to the needs of others. Self-interest is a universal trait found amongst socialist nations as much as capitalist, particularly with respect to socialist dictators who plunder the country for their own benefit. The willingness not to consume, but to risk and create is the distinction of capitalism. The entrepreneur is the producer of the wealth of everyone else. He invests his own foregone consumption in products that people may or may not want, before he gets any return. He spends money on wages and inventory and other operating costs, before he receives any return, being motivated less by the desire to consume, than the desire to create. Business owners are no greedier or more self-interested than doctors or writers or sociologists or government officials but they are impelled by faith in the world outside themselves.

Entrepreneurs should be able to maintain their wealth because only they know how best to invest it out of a vast array of business opportunities. Without retained income and profits, businesses cannot be flexible and seek out new ways to grow and expand wealth. This function is essential to the employment and welfare of the whole nation. The person who hoards wealth, on the other hand, is not a capitalist, nor is he or she creating anything. Neither is such a person an owner of productive capital. Socialist welfare destroys the idea of having to help others in order to help oneself. The "me" generation wants the security of the welfare state, but will not reach beyond themselves like the capitalist. So its socialism that exalts greed, not capitalism. Greed is wanting other people to support you without contributing anything to them.

The Free Market is about Creativity

Adam Smith focused on the division of labour and incentives but he missed the creative aspect of capitalism, which Gilder picks up on (Gregorsky 1998 292). Capitalism is not just about an efficient allocation of existing resources, though it does that very well, its about creating completely new things. The entrepreneur must look at the future imaginatively and create new market, new products, he must be creative in meeting our needs.

The Free market is about Freedom

In the words of Reisman again:

> "Individual freedom—an essential feature of capitalism—is *the foundation of security,* in the sense both of personal safety and of economic security. Freedom means *the absence of the initiation of physical force.* When one is free, one is safe—secure—from common crime, because what one is free of or free from is precisely acts such as assault and battery, robbery, rape, and murder, all of which represent the initiation of physical force. Even more important, of course, is that when one is free, one is free from the initiation of physical force on the part of *the government*, which is potentially far more deadly than that of any private criminal gang. (The Gestapo and the KGB, for example, with their enslavement and murder of millions made private criminals look almost kind by comparison.)
>
> …The *economic security* provided by freedom derives from the fact that under freedom, everyone can choose to do whatever he judges to be most in his own interest, without fear of being stopped by the physical force of anyone else, so long as he himself does not initiate the use of physical force. This means, for example, that he can take the highest paying job he can find and buy from the most competitive suppliers he can find; at the same time, he can keep all the income he earns and save as much of it as he likes, investing his savings in the most profitable ways he can. The only thing he cannot do is use force

himself. With the use of force prohibited, the way an individual increases the money he earns is by using his reason to figure out how to offer other people more or better goods and services for the same money. This is the means of inducing them voluntarily to spend more of their funds in buying from him rather than from competitors. Thus, freedom is the basis of everyone being as economically secure as the exercise of his own reason and the reason of his suppliers can make him." (Reisman 2002)

Gray and other detractors of capitalism, on the other hand, clearly do not consider freedom important at all (Gray, 1998: 108) since every state program they defend or advocate inevitably decreases the freedom of every citizen.

Sin is not in the capitalist system, it is in the nature of man.

Does money make people selfish or are people selfish to start with? For a Christian there should be no debate, it is biblically clear that everyone is intrinsically sinful, that is where the world's problems come from. This has been the moral backdrop of the West for centuries. Money is just a measure of the value people place on things; it is a means of exchange. People do not sacrifice their families on the alter of materialism because there is something wrong with money, but because there is something wrong with people.

The love of money is a human condition, it is not because there is anything wrong with money but rather whether your attitude is right. Of course during bull markets and stock market bubbles, some people become absorbed with chasing financial gain to such as degree they make it an ideal. This is the fault of the individual not the system. "Bear markets correct not only stock prices, but attitudes and philosophies. People turn away from the existential pleasures of "Getting rich NOW!" in favour of other things. They turn to gardening. They begin to think about history or read mystery stories. They begin to think about what real value really is. Their values correct. Other people could have made money in the bull market without it being the centre of their life, having the right attitude." The system (or the devil) does not make them do it, we can choose (Bonner 2002).

Gray(1998: 38) thinks that the free market destroys virtues. This is simply historically not the case. The Victorian Era, America in the first half of the 20th century, Korea today, and Holland in the 16th century were all not only the most free market areas but the most morally and ethically concerned as well. It is socialism and government control that erode morality. His argument is not grounded on the facts.

Rebels Without a Clue?

The Free Market works when people are wicked (unlike socialism) but works even better when people are good (unlike socialism)

One of the wonderful features of the free market is that it is both realistic and inspiring. Realistic because it takes into account the Christian doctrine of the sinful condition of mankind. Therefore, socialism, by positing the goodness of man (against all the evidence, of course) expects civil servants who have nothing to gain from efficiency to be as keen to serve as businessmen who have everything to gain from keeping their customers satisfied. It is this wrong premise that is much of the reason why Socialism does not work and the free market does.

But it is not just a practical matter that makes Freedom a superior system; it is the opportunities that it gives you. Therefore, socialism ties everyone up with rules and regulations, it takes away your opportunity through taxation and state power. Only the state is free, everyone else is in chains. The free market on the other hand gives you the opportunity to be as effective as possible, to really serve others. It gives you the financial freedom to be idealistic, to be all you can be for God, to be and do what He created you to do.

The fact that capitalism is all about giving and idealism and altruism by its very nature is one of George Gilder's themes. Ayn Rand and more classic libertarians might disagree with this focusing on how the market enables even selfish people to work together. Bringing the two together means that the market will work even when people are bad, but it will work even better when people are willing to give to others especially through investment and entrepreneurship.

Not realizing that capitalism is an altruistic system and almost idealising selfishness, is one of the few errors in Rand's thinking. So for people who are inclined to be bad, Freedom is the better system and for people who want to do the right thing, the Free Market will also give them the ability to do it. Socialism fails on both counts.

Should we make the world even more imperfect by ignoring market solutions? Sometimes people unfamiliar with market dynamics suggest that the free market is all very well for a perfect world but would not work in real life. Therefore, socialism is required to cope with the world as it really is. John Gray does not seem to know what he believes, arguing that both the free market and socialism are utopian! (Gray, 1998: 2-3).

The idea that free markets are utopian is inaccurate and ironic for a number of reasons.
1. Socialism is known as a utopian ideology, and it is self consciously so. Its main power is to hold out a (false) ideal and then try and get reality to follow.

Rebels Without a Clue?

Therefore, it is socialism (involving governments in economic life) that is not right for the real world.

2. The free market again and again, in hundreds of countries and multitudes of time periods and situations been proven beyond reasonable doubt to be a very practical system. It works and few doubt it. Even socialist countries keep a section of their countries capitalist so they can keep their people alive. They know government management does not work. They are simply interested in maintaining their own power.
3. Even when free market principles are applied beyond the realms we normally understand them operating in, we know it will work because it is the same thing that has worked in every other area, and human nature does not change. Economic laws are like the laws of gravity and thermodynamics. It is realistic to expect them to work everywhere.
4. The free market is designed for imperfection - not perfect worlds. Its beauty is that it will make even wicked people serve one another in order to make a living. Government can try and force wicked people to serve their purposes but this does not work as well as the free market does through voluntary means.
5. The Russian system and others were ineffective not because they were based on an ideal (Utopian) but because they were based on a wrong ideal (socialism). We cannot argue that the free market should be moderated because the idealistic application of its opposite did not work!
6. In a perfect world, the free market would not be needed. As Winston Churchill once said "There are two places where socialism would work: heaven, where they do not need it ….and hell where they have already got it!"

Socialism and Communism are in practice exactly the same thing

Neither can we distinguish between communism and socialism. The two words are used interchangeably in all socialist countries. The 19th century founders of the movement used the terms interchangeably. What is the difference between these policies? Both terms imply a state with lots of taxes and lots of power. These are the kinds of states that can perpetrate atrocities — both against its citizens and whoever is thought to be against them. There is no link between this statement and the paragraph! Repeat from above. Reading the dreadful stories above, every moral or intelligent person should be totally in favour of the free market. Therefore, socialism is evil - there is no other way to put it.

Rebels Without a Clue?

Socialists have killed millions of innocent people

In the name of the working class, socialist leaders of the USSR, Mozambique, Angola, Rwanda, China, and Cuba literally killed millions of innocent people and caused many more to starve in order to pad their personal bank accounts. National Socialism in Hitler's Germany killed millions of Jews internally and caused the deaths of millions more globally because people believed in socialism. If people had acted on the free market belief that the state should have very little power then neither Stalin nor Hitler nor any other socialists would have been able to do what they did. This in itself should be enough to ensure that any moral person does not believe in socialism.

This is not simply a problem of evil men, since there will always be evil men, but a question of restraints in the system. To put socialism into practice, the state requires a free hand, which has regularly enabled evil men to abuse this power. With a tax-free society, there is no money for governments to divert for their own nefarious purposes as it would all be in the hands of private entrepreneurs, who would only be abusing their own money, and are not known for financing private armies! Thus the corruption in Africa is primarily a systemic failure. The only solution is to downsize the state so there is no power to abuse! What is needed is less power in the hands of government, rather than the perceived need for good government.

So let us not beat around the bush. By believing and promoting a system in which the state has power to tax, socialists around the world, have enabled the killing of millions of innocent people. Repenting from this horrible ideology and adopting a moral, free market way of thinking where governments have no power to do these kinds of things is the only way to stop these horrible things happening again. Let's not delude ourselves.

Unofficial Estimates of the Murder Rate of Socialist governments in the 20th century	
USSR	20 million
China	65 million
Vietnam	1 million
North Korea	2 million
Cambodia	2 million
Eastern Europe	1 million
Latin America	150,000
Africa	1.7 million
Afghanistan	1.5 million

Rebels Without a Clue?

International Communist parties not in power	10,000 deaths
The total approaches 100 million people killed.	

Source: Black book of communism: p4

The USSR, the first of the Communist regimes, did not just commit criminal acts (all states do so on occasion); they were criminal enterprises in their very essence. On principle, so to speak, they all ruled lawlessly, by violence and without regard for human life.

According to Stephan Courtois, a prominent French historian:

> "[T]here never was a benign, initial phase of Communism before some mythical 'wrong turn' threw it off track. From the start Lenin expected, indeed wanted, civil war to crush all 'class enemies', and this war, principally against the peasants, continued with only short pauses until 1953. Therefore, much for the fable of 'good Lenin/bad Stalin'...Communism's recourse to 'permanent civil war' rested on the 'scientific' Marxist belief in class struggle as the 'violent midwife of history', in Marx's famous metaphor."

From these atrocities, which represent the smallest fraction, how can anybody conclude that socialism is good for the poor? We cannot allow ourselves the intellectual argument that while socialism was bad in most of the countries in which it was applied, our countries should move towards a more socialist structure. The risks are too great!

Socialism and the destruction of human capital

Socialism is a way of destroying your best people or at least destroying their production. Therefore, socialism does not tolerate anyone to rise above the herd, never mind be rewarded for doing to. Therefore, we loose the benefits of our best people's production. Under Hitler's National Socialism, Germany lost many of its best scientists to America, particularly the Jews. Any of Ayn Rand's exceedingly well written novels demonstrate the destruction of people through socialism. Contrary to those who claim to represent "human rights rather than property rights", socialism destroys both, whereas capitalism protects both. Property rights in any case accrue to humans and are necessary to exercise most human rights. You only have freedom of speech or assembly on your own or friendly property. How do you have no freedom of the press if the government owns it (Rothbard, 1970: 238).

Rebels Without a Clue?

One should note here that when we are talking about socialism we are not just talking about far off events in Russia or China but any time a government runs an activity, be it education, health, policing or housing we are seeing socialism with all its defects.

Common Misconception: Is it all about Money?

No. It is all about Freedom. It is all about Responsibility. It is all about serving other people. And, if you can trace the consequences a few steps beyond the obvious, compassion plays at least as big a role in free market societies as in socialist ones. The free market is the only way the poorest people in society have ever become rich.

When you discuss for a length of time the various free market mechanisms designed to make education better and cheaper, or building regulations work by tradable property rights rather than bureaucrats spending taxes, it may seem that we are making the world revolve round money. There are various reasons why this is not an accurate understanding:

Whichever way things are ordered, markets or governments, and whatever area of life we are deciding who should run, the funding of it is inevitably about money. If money is collected in taxes and spent then it is no less material than if you and I spend it in the market for healthcare or groceries. The free market then is no more about money than socialist decision-making processes. Socialism is self consciously materialistic. Its root philosophy is called dialectic materialism. Marx believed in economic determinism. In other words he would have told you quite definitely that "its all about money". The free market with its Christian historical roots, on the other hand, has always affirmed money as good, but as subordinate to greater goods: God's will, good families, changing the world. If you doubt that read Max Weber's classic "The Protestant Work Ethic and the Spirit of Capitalism". Consider also that in each time period the greatest missionary sending nations have also been the freest market: UK in the 19th century, the US in the first half of the 20th and South Korea today. Free market nations have always valued the family. Marx on the other hand (and Plato) was hostile to the family and wanted the state to bring up children. Thus we can see that the free market, by dealing effectively with economic matters, leaves people free to concentrate on the higher things in life.

Related to this area is the idea that people should be able to decide about other people's property through a democratically elected group or social construct. This is no more or less about money than deciding through market processes. However, this

Rebels Without a Clue?

time it is about other people's money not voluntarily given funds. This is morally dubious (it could be seen as a form of theft) and destroys the incentives for effective wealth management (people generally spend other people's wealth a little more freely than their own).

Power issues related to this also arise. Is it a problem if a few rich people dominate some local decision making process because they are more wealthy? Some people think it might be a significant problem in a pure free market economy. I'm not so sure it would be such a big deal most of the time. In a government structure, small numbers of people dominate local processes also. They do this much more comprehensively and destructively than private capital ever could. This is because they have money, just like the rich capitalist, but they have more than money, they also have legal power. Therefore, while concentrations may arise, the resulting problem is less than with a government system. All we can ever hope for is a better system, not a perfect system. And market systems are better than government ones.

Furthermore, it is very hard for one person to dominate a local issue no matter how rich he is. Even for a man worth a million dollars, it would only take a combination of 100 people worth 10,000 dollars to equal his financial power and a community of 10,000 such people would have the same financial clout as a man worth 100 million dollars.

There is no doubt that sometimes decisions would be made by corporations and individuals that would upset communities from time to time. This is just part of life. However, there is also no doubt that these instances would be less than under the irrational, virtually unaccountable, political world of government, whatever its structure and size.

Similarly, the idea that people are more important than things is true of all Christian free markets. Therefore, socialism and capitalism both are systems where things are made. Whether people are more important to other people is a condition of these people's hearts, not a question of systems.

Common Misconception: Is Socialism about groups and Capitalism about individuals?

People often send me examples of people working together to achieve an objective. Therefore, sometimes these are inspiring, showing the power of faith communities in achieving social objectives. The problem is that this sometimes comes with a note that implies that this proves that socialism works. This is a bit strange as these are always examples of voluntary associations not the power of the state. This is not an example of a balance between capitalism and socialism but between individuals and groups within free capitalism. Capitalism is not against people doing things in groups. This is indeed the essence of a corporation.

Rebels Without a Clue?

The difference between Capitalism and Socialism is that Socialism makes people do things in groups by coercion. It is a form of theft and envy, antithetical to ethics. It reduces the 8th commandment to "thou shalt not steal, except by majority vote" That "man is a social animal" is not an argument for the state to do anything. It is an argument for people to do things in groups. (See Rothbard 1970: 237+ for a refutation of Rommen's arguments in this context.) The state being based on force is an anti-social organisation. For extended families to help each other when they are in trouble is as much part of a free market where power is returned from the state to families as anything else. The decline of this in the West is probably more to do with its retreat from its previously Christian ideology than its adoption of the market. Its decline in any case has followed its adoption of more socialist policies, most of which have still not been reversed.

Common Misconception: Is "unbridled" or "cutthroat" competition really something to be avoided?

People often advance a socialist agenda by talking about "unbridled" or "cutthroat" competition and use these phrases to justify state intervention. This is spurious. That which is called cut throat competition is really cut *price* competition. It is people trying extremely hard to get give you the best deal so that they can benefit from your business. Unless one is a butcher, it is very rare for one to cut throats in business. Far less common in fact than it has been in the socialist utopias the anti-capitalists want us to emulate. In this connection we should bear in mind that the free market does not mean the will of the corporates. In fact national associations of employers often exist simply to resist competition (Rand, 1957: 72)

Competition is a great process and the last thing we should want is for the government to reduce the effectiveness of this process by taxing or regulating. If any particular business is doing something illegal of course, then that should be dealt with individually by a network of efficient private courts. However, it would never be a reason to reduce competition in the system.

Reich discusses the rise of oligarchic corporations in the US in the middle of the twentieth century who prevent "fly by night" competitors and thus "protect" the consumer (Reich, 2002: 16). However, preventing competition is a bad thing for the same reasons that the rise in flexibility, and markets with a greater amount of competition is a good thing. Small companies, a few of whom may turn out for various reasons to be "fly by night", are anyway helping to bring down prices for everyone by their selling of products and services in the market place.

Rebels Without a Clue?

Should business have a "social conscience"?

Business in general does a huge amount of good in charitable work not related to their main business. Because of the efficiency with which they do it, they often accomplish more than governments -which is the way it should be. The generosity of businesses in this respect should not blind us to the fact that businesses as a group do infinitely more for society in their normal line of commercial activities than in any charitable activities that they could possibly do. The normal business of continually improving products and cutting prices is what raises the standard of living for society as a whole. It is what entrepreneurs do in their work time not primarily their spare time that improves the lifestyles of the poor of a country through the lower prices of products. Therefore, in a way, if all businesses stopped being commercial and applied themselves to widows and orphans in a charitable sense, they would probably do less good for the widows and orphans than they would if they did no so called "social concern" projects and simply concentrated on bringing down prices and bringing up quality in their sector. To put it succinctly, business itself results in charitable activity. Just because that is not their motives does not mean it is not their effect.

Connected to the above is the idea of businesses as welfare institutions, for example, in one of its manifestations, the idea that businesses exist to give jobs to their workers, is an idea still popular in Japan. The problem with this is that by keeping workers they do not need, they necessarily keep the prices of their products up - beyond what they would otherwise be. This is a major social cost especially to the poor. Therefore, ironically, sometimes the most seemingly nasty businesses and business processes where lots of people loose their jobs are really doing the best for the poor by bringing down prices for them most quickly! In economics, it is always necessary to look below the surface.

The idea that business is for "public service not profit" is another misunderstanding. In a competitive market, public service is demonstrated by profits. The ones who serve the need best get the business. People mustn't think they are delivering a service of value to the public if they are not profitable. If they are loosing money it means that the public does not value their service! This would apply to services in rural areas as a public service when it is not profitable. People (especially in the West) can be rural and not poor and city dwellers can be poor too. Therefore, why we should subsidise ruralness in itself is not obvious.

The mirror image of this is that labour laws of any kind, which ignorant people generally think are good for the poor, but actually price the unskilled out of the market. By raising costs for businesses and therefore prices in the market they lower the standard of living of the poor. In the words of George Gilder, profits are an "index of altruism", a measure of how much you are helping people (Gregorsky, 1998: 113)

Rebels Without a Clue?

Claiming something is "owned by the people" usually means it has been stolen from one of them. When something is valuable, wicked people often try to steal it for their own interests by saying it belongs to "the people" or to "mankind" when really it belongs to the owner. If we are serious that theft should not be allowed, we must be clear that nothing belongs to the people as an entity. Things can only belong to individuals and to groups of individuals. Saying that things belong to "the people" means that no one owns it and so no one will look after it.

Common Misconception: Do people have an inherent right to Sponge?

From his discussion of the Poor Laws Gray (1998: 10) he shows that he does not believe that a man should be expected to contribute to the community by working. He should be supported by the community rather than take a low paying job. The Bible on the other hand, hardly a book unconcerned with compassion says "if a "man shall not work, he shall not eat" (2 Thessalonians 3: 10) It is people like Gray who are responsible for a lost generation in the West who have never worked, who are rationally unprepared (thanks to the Welfare state he supports) to start at the bottom and work their way up. Being unprepared to serve others is not a social virtue. His argument that people should not have to work and serve others if the wage is too low is, to be frank, appalling.

Common Misconception: Are people becoming more selfish and less loyal?

Once again, even some of the socialist writers understand this is not the case. One of the central theses of Reich's "Future of Success" (e.g. 1991 71) is that people's attitudes haven't changed, it is just that in a more market based economy people get paid what they are worth and so the incentives to move to a different company are proportionately greater. The important thing to understand is that loyalty in the sense of security of employment for the employee, or guarantee that your employees will stay in the case of the employer is not an obligation of either party. The idea of a steady job is in any case a historical anomaly, starting only in the industrial revolution, before which people produced as small businesses effectively, which is what we are going back to today.[2]

Loyalty is due to our families and our friends. In the workplace, it is better for society as a whole if people rapidly move to the company and position where they can create the most value for society as a whole. The value people create for others is reflected in their remuneration. In other words, the constant search for the better deal by

---

2 For more on "Who protects the worker" see the 20 page discussion in Friedman (1979: 228).

individuals and companies is a positive social process that leads to better goods and services for you and me, and cheaper goods and services for the less well off members of the community who need it most.

However, that does not mean that there is no loyalty. Particular people will work well together and become good friends. Permanent teams will form. The people that I work with in many cases will still work for me in years to come. Like a marriage, when you work with people for a long time, you have an investment in understanding how they work, and vice versa, that is not easily replicated. Therefore, loyalty still makes sense, and always will, but in a personal way, to people, not in an impersonal way to a corporation. High personal loyalty in the new economy means people come as packages with their support staff, or as highly technical teams that work together. Loyalty has changed but it is not been abolished.

Common Misconception: Are eroding wages for workers inevitable?

All this means, to Reich, is that workers do worse than before. However, even if their wages and benefits do fall they are able to buy more with it because the corporate restructuring and lay offs and benefit cuts make the things that they buy cheaper. Therefore, although their nominal wages and benefits may be falling, the price of what they buy is falling still faster (or rising less fast than it would otherwise be rising.) Companies have profits of 5% of the cost of the goods. By far the largest proportion of the price that we pay goes to paying employees .In fact, in most economies around 80% of the price we pay for goods goes to workers, with the other 15% being investment. Therefore, if wages are falling, in a competitive economy, the prices of products must be failing to.

The other side of falling wages, is that some of the benefits they had before were illegitimate, coerced by force by unions threatening strikes and disruptions from corporations and thus from the consumers that bought the final, more expensive, product. This might have been great for high wage blue-collar workers, but it was not so good for the end user who is an old lady in a cold housing scheme in Chicago or Aberdeen or Warsaw wondering why the gas to heat her house is so expensive.

Inequality

Bill Gates is allegedly worth as much as the bottom 50% of the US population, and the top 1% worth as much as the bottom 100 million. I am not sure if this takes into account recent stock market falls. However we should remember that, leaving Gates, aside for now, that the top 1% have created huge value for the US population without whom they would have no jobs and no products to buy. If they left the country or all their money was taken from them, most of the US economy would be gone! They are the ones with the expertise that makes the US economy different from the lowest economies in the world. It is not the bottom 50% that have risked, strategised, put deals together, read, studied, and understood. They have just drifted into work every day and done what they were told. It is fine to do that if that is what one chooses to do but the people that make the wealth of the whole of America actually happen, should be seen, in general, as good people, people to be rather admired than envied. There are notorious exceptions of course but largely the wealthiest 1% has done a tremendous amount for the poor, for you and for everyone in society.

Inequality may have been caused more simply by new technologies that only a small number have so far mastered rather than policy. The first people to learn a new technology become richer quicker, then things equalise later, so in other words it is not necessarily a long-term trend. Reich uses the weasel words of relative inequality that is an envy base measure to try to make the situation for the poor look worse than it is (Reich, 2002: 102,107). If the absolute incomes of the poor are rising faster than they otherwise would be, it is not an issue if the incomes of the rich are rising faster. To say that it is an issue is to say that what we want is not the good of the poor but simply to destroy the successful. Therefore, societies that think like this, end up destroyed.

The poor are definitely not getting poorer in the West if you look at what they can now afford. They now have inexpensive long distance telephony, mobile phones, drugs to control hypertension and they have had for a long time: air conditioning, cars and by world standards, good housing. Air line tickets, TVs, computers, videos, cameras, effective cancer treatment, and a host of other things are much cheaper than they were -which Reich points out (2002: 161). Of course much more could be done in terms of privatising education, health, policing, courts and roads, and thus lowering the taxes that put up the prices on everything they buy, to improve their condition. Socialists do not seem to usually want to help them in this effective a way.

Inequality amongst graduate students as well (cited by Reich) is not necessarily a bad thing. To some degree, it is simply a refection of how hard people work, what people skills they have developed, their character and their discipline. It is not to a large degree, a social problem.

Gray makes much of rising inequality in the US (Gray,1998: 114) (see also Turner,2001: 84) though I suspect the dates (ending in 1995) might make his point less forcibly if they ended today. What he has noted is that the income of the bottom 60% fell by 3.2% from 34.9% to 31.7% and the top fifth received that gain. He argues that this amount is significant, though a 10% rise in income would not do that much good for the poor in my opinion. However, he ignores the fact that the efficiency

Rebels Without a Clue?

generated by this shift probably generated more economic growth that would have helped many of the bottom 60%, in addition to making the prices of things cheaper which, again, makes the poor richer even if their earnings are not nominally going up. Furthermore, this is a once off adjustment as those who were being stolen from before receive the full value of their production. It also helps those in previously protected jobs adjust to employment that adds more value to everyone else. Most importantly of all though is the cost of the many socialist regulations and government enterprises and departments that are the main place where all the money of the poor and middle class are going. Privatisation of the remaining 30% of the economy left with the government in the US would do much more to raise incomes for everyone than any anti capitalist measure.

Similarly if the "sorting mechanism" (Reich 2002 207) means that more healthy people get cheaper insurance and the less healthy have to pay more then it is not a bad thing if people have still greater incentives to adopt healthy life styles, not just for themselves, but also for their families, their friends and for society as a whole. Health/ill health is not necessarily a rich/poor thing but even the cases where it is, if is necessary to redistribute at all, it is not clear why we should do it in such a way as it gives incentives to people to be unhealthy.

Inequality, contrary to popular belief, is often higher in socialist or ex socialist countries. Even Gray relates: "inequality in Dengist [mainland communist] China is almost certainly greater than in an unequivocally capitalist country like Taiwan" (1998 185) In the Cold War era the most unequal part of the world were the socialist ones, particularly Mexico and Brazil.
In other words, even if inequality in itself is seen as a problem, socialism is not the solution!

Common Misconception: Winner takes all: "We all go together or a few become rich and the rest are left behind?"
The problems with this statement, is that usually in any major technological change a few adjust and then others copy them, so there is a widening then a narrowing of inequality and that is OK. Secondly, we need to have incentives for everyone to make the changes and adjust so they do not get left behind, a flexible free market in the best way to do this.

Common Misconception: Does most of the money in society go to greedy businessmen and investors who are all rich?

Socialism tells us that businessmen greedily take all the money in profits. "If only" say most businessmen. However, the facts are the facts: "Corporate profits of the non-financial sector in the US as a whole, peaked in the second quarter of 2000 at $518 billion, annualised," Richebacher observes. "By the fourth quarter of 2001, they were down 44.4%, to $287.7 billion" (Bonner 2002).

Out of a $10 trillion dollar economy that's, 5% and 3% respectively, hardly a high percentage of the total cake. The rest goes mostly to labour. The truth is that capitalism through competition allocates most the proceeds from sales to its employees, at least 80%. Businessmen do not usually do this out of the goodness of their hearts. It is forced on them by a market economy. This is in fact, another social benefit of the free market. In more statist societies like feudalism, the elite can control a far higher percentage of the total cake. According to Gregory King's statistics in 1688, the nobility in England at that time controlled about 50% of the income of the country.

Furthermore, for all the concentration of power in corporations that socialists errantly talk about, there is doubtless far more power concentrated in governments. That is the bigger problem! And unlike Government, the funds of corporations come back to us either in cheaper products or in share dividends and capital gains in our pensions and investment portfolios.

Why businessmen cannot get away with paying less than the just wage.

Socialists sometimes argue that employers exploit labour by paying them less than the correct rate. They would if they could, of course, just as many workers would prefer not to have to pay for what they buy, but thankfully, it is quite impossible! Reisman relates:

> "Capitalism is a system of progressively rising real wages, the shortening of hours, and the improvement of working conditions. The fact that wage earners may be willing to work for minimum subsistence, in the absence of any better alternative, and that businessmen and capitalists, like any other buyer, prefer to pay less rather than more, are propositions that are true but utterly irrelevant to the determination of the wages that the wage earners must actually accept. Those wages are determined by the competition of employers for labour, which is both the most fundamentally useful element in the economic system and is intrinsically scarce.
>
> In that competition, it is against the self-interest of any employer to allow wage rates to go below the point corresponding to the full employment of the kind of labour in question, in the location in question. Such low wage rates mean that the quantity of labour demanded exceeds the supply available, i.e., that there is a

shortage of the labour concerned. A shortage of labour is comparable to an auction in which there are still two or more bidders for one and the same item. The only way that the bidder who wants the item the most can secure it, is by outbidding his rivals and making the item too expensive for them, so that they must step aside and make it possible for him to secure the item.

In the labour market there may be tens or even hundreds of millions of workers. However, the scarcity of labour means that there are potential jobs for far more than that number. The fact that each of us would like the benefit of the labour of at least ten others can be taken as an indication of the extent of the scarcity of labour.

When a wage rate goes below the point corresponding to the full employment of the kind of labour concerned, it becomes possible for employers not able or willing to pay that higher rate to obtain labour at the expense of other employers who are able and willing to pay that higher rate. The situation is exactly the same as the stronger bidder at an auction who is faced with the loss of the item he wants to another, weaker bidder. The way to secure the labour he needs is to raise the bidding and knock out the competition of the weaker employers.

In the face of labour shortages, which appear when ceiling prices are imposed on labour, employers actually conspire with their employees to evade the spirit of the wage controls, by giving out phoney promotions. The promotion allows employers to pay higher wages to attract workers than would normally be allowed under the guise that they are managers. This enables them to claim that they are not violating the controls when in fact they are.

Now, given the height of money wage rates, which we have seen is determined by the competition of employers for scarce labour, what determines *real* wages, i.e., the goods and services that the wage earners can buy with the money they earn, is *prices*. Real wages are determined fully as much by prices as they are by wages. Real wages rise only when prices fall relative to wages.

What makes prices fall relative to wages is a rise in the productivity of labour, i.e., the output per unit of labour. A rise in the productivity of labour means a larger supply of consumers goods relative to the supply of labour, and thus lower prices of consumers' goods relative to

43

wage rates. If we could somehow measure the supply of consumers' goods, a doubling of the productivity of labour would operate to double the supply of consumers' goods relative to the supply of labour and, in the face of the same overall respective expenditures to buy consumers' goods and labour, result in a halving of the prices of consumers' goods in the face of the same overall average wage rates. In other words, it would double real wage rates.

And what is responsible for the rise in the productivity of labour is the activities of businessmen and capitalists. Their progressive innovations and capital accumulation underlie the rise in the productivity of labour and thus in real wages." For further discussion on the illogical nature of alternative theories of just wages see Hayek (1944 76+).

Socialism is not simply wrong it is a deception

Real evil is deceptive in its nature. It makes sense for evil to be so – for if men were presented with the real nature of evil, very few would take part in it. Therefore, evil disguises itself well and poses "as an angel of light" (2 Corinthians 11: 14-15) so that it may deceive men.

Socialism masquerades as a great good – especially for the poor. It taps into the very fears and prejudices of the worst side of mankind. Indeed, Socialism is intended to reach and convert two groups of people. There are those diabolically wise enough to understand that Socialism can make them rich – especially if they are employed by the State. For as profits are confiscated and property is taken from its individual owners into the fold of State assets, so they become the partial recipients. For even if nobody owns anything in the Socialist State, somebody must administer land, taxes, profits and so on. The ideal of wealth redistribution is left behind as the fat cats at the top line their pockets. This must be taken into account when people hear the call for redistribution!

The second group of people is made up of those that understand very little – but are duped by the false promises and deceptively high ideals of socialism, and are too stupid or lazy to discover the true nature of Socialism (Dembovsky 2002)

Killing the Golden Goose: socialism by forced sharing destroys what there is to share. Socialism creates a society where nothing works, nothing arrives on time, nothing is good and nothing is value for money. In a socialist society (or a government run area in a free country), no one has an incentive to produce so the amount of things produced reduces dramatically in quality and quantity. This means there is less value to redistribute (steal). Inevitably then, however equal, in a socialist society everyone has less. A good demonstration of this in novel form that everyone

Rebels Without a Clue?

should read is Ayn Rand's "We the Living" and she experienced it first hand growing up in Russia after the revolution (Rand: 1936).

Common Misconception : Can the state improve character better than freedom?

"Human welfare is more than GDP/capita statistics" (response to Turner 2001 5) "Success depends on our spiritual grounding, the richness of our relationships, the sturdiness of our families and the character of our communities" (Reich 2002 248) These quotations are certainly true. However, their implications are misleading to a certain degree. Many of the things that would be included in human welfare but not GDP/stats could be best helped by an extension of the free market to these areas: that would include the atmosphere, parks, noise, etc. Human welfare also includes people's beliefs and character, and their connection to God, their families and the community. Some of these things are personal responsibilities that cannot come from any economic system. However, to the degree to which they can be influenced by the system, the free market is the best system. Therefore, socialism does not lead to character formation and spirituality in education as much as private systems always have historically. The character formation of free institutions like churches and (historically) friendly societies were entirely lacking in the Eastern Block socialist systems. Parks, rivers and the environment were polluted dreadfully when governments were allowed free reign in these countries. Certainly, there is more to human welfare than GDP statistics but that's a reason for more privatisation, not les.

Litter and sexual harassment are symptoms of government ownership

Litter is only a problem in public areas, in case you hadn't noticed. In cinemas, there is no litter - only rubbish that is picked up by cleaners at the end of every show. There is no litter in restaurants because it is picked up or cleaned up when the customers leave. In private hospitals rubbish is picked up right away in order to preserve a clean environment. If all areas were owned privately, they would be cleaned by their owners and that costs would be bourn by the litterer in their park entrance fee or street tolls. Non customers littering without paying would be sued or asked to leave. Littering is a problem that only exists because no one owns the place being littered (or the government owns it which comes to the same thing, as governments do not have the incentives or resources to fix the problem).

Another problem that may be of interest to the women's movement or to women in general is the incidence of verbal harassment, unwanted flirting and whistling. Why does this happen mostly in (government owned) streets and not really in (privately owned) restaurants, department stores and malls. The answer is of course that the owners of these venues have the incentive to make sure their customers do not get harassed. The solution then is to privatise city streets and parks, so that their owners, wanting you to use their particular streets and parks, will ensure a pleasant walking environment for women.

Similarly, in the case of sexual harassment at work, a private employer will loose money if he harasses his employees through transaction costs from rapid turnover, through having to make do with less productive people or through having to pay people more to stay. Thus the free market discourages sexual harassments through its competitive markets.
On the other hand, if the state is employing it looses nothing when this kind of activity goes on, so it will happen more. We do not hear of many discrimination suits from the advertising or computer industries, being mostly private but from government sectors like teaching, social work and libraries. The only solution is to privatise these activities so that governments are no longer involved here.
(As an aside, it is also significant that most occurrences of women getting different pay from men happen in the government sector. In the private sector, no one can afford to let good female employees go.)

Even the socialists admit that the free market revolution of the last 20 years has given rise to "significant numbers" of every gender and race becoming part of corporate boardrooms (Reich 2002 140). The free market only cares about how good you are at you job. Therefore, socialist bureaucrats have the freedom to express their preferences, however much we might object. More free market pressures will solve the problem more completely, as there is still a long way to go.

Working on the basis of need rather than merit

"To each, according to his needs, from each according to his ability"
It may sound good when first heard but with a bit of analysis it is clearly not remotely just. People should get according to their merits and their contribution to others, not in terms of their needs. It is true that people should get according to their ability but also according to their application and their willingness to step out in faith and take risks. The problem on the second half of the saying is that people will not contribute according to their ability if they are not getting in proportion to their contribution but according to some vaguely defined concept of need.
Finally, there is a practical difficulty. If we are rewarded according to how other people value our contribution (the market) we do not need any kind of intermediately, we have a normal buying/selling transaction. On the other hand, if we are to be rewarded by the rest of the people in our society on the basis of our need then we need a third party to decide what everybody's need is. In other words it is an intensely impractical system.
More than that though, it is also an unjust system, because the person that has to decide whose need is greatest has no objective way of deciding. Even if he did know,

he would be very open to bribes. The subjectivity of the task would create dreadfully demotivated people that cannot do better by working harder or contributing more. Connected to the argument above is the thought that those who steal to feed a hungry family should not be punished. In the extreme case the law would also be on the side of the thief, the defence is known as "necessity". However the extreme case is rather rare, even in Africa. Most people may be poor but they have enough to eat without starving and in famine situations there is no one to steal from.
However, poverty without necessity can never be a justification for theft, especially since most of those who are stolen from are also poor, and the regular thief in a poor community usually has an income a good deal higher than the average honest person in that community. Most people however poor, are not thieves. Being pro thief is not being pro poor.

The balance of power

To the disgust of Thomas Frank, in his book "One Market under God", describes the message of Rush Limbaugh and the American Right – that socialism and the left is all about the elites telling ordinary people what to do – as opposed to a market system where the people decide by who they give their custom to.. Regulatory systems create elites. Government departments create elites. Getting rid of these guys really is "power to the people" in a way communism never was. Therefore, socialism is power to the (alleged) representatives of the people, not to the actual people themselves.

That's not to say that I agree with the populist position associated with justifications for democracy that "the people" are intelligent and there is no such thing as high culture (Frank, 2000: 282.) It is well known that Intelligence is on a bell curve (especially Charles Murray) (Herrnstein 1994) and the culture directed as the lower segment of that curve will be less intelligent. That does not mean its equal to higher culture but neither should it be banned. It is not a problem with the market that it can cater to all tastes, it is an advantage.

Chapter 3

How Markets work and why they are better than Socialism

Why is the private sector more efficient?

Protecting industries has never worked. For example, protecting Europe's high technology industry only caused it to be overtaken by more streamlined American companies. Korea is now facing the consequences of having created huge protected companies; which were to some degree, insulated from the market. Japan too, may be regretting this policy of protectionism. Many previously protected industries in Africa now have had to be shut down entirely.

It is now a settled issue that previously nationalised companies that are exposed to the rigours of a genuinely competitive market produce goods and services at a far cheaper price than their government-run equivalents. A famous 1971 study showed that it cost cities (in this case New York) 2.6 times as much as the private sector to provide services like the paving of streets and collection of trash. This is valid for schools, hospitals as well as telecommunications and electricity.

Large-scale scientific studies in the USA, Canada and Switzerland conclusively demonstrate that it costs the public at least 30-40% more when government provides the service directly rather than by contracts with private firms (and even the latter only partially realises the benefits of full privatisation). For example, janitorial services cost 73% more, street cleaning cost 43% more, paving cost 96% more and the maintenance of traffic lights cost 56% more. Governments have no incentive to control costs. In Africa, these savings would be much greater because governments have even less incentives and resources than in the west and business needs to be even leaner in order to survive.

Incentives

The reason why the private sector is more efficient than anything run by the government is primarily concerned with incentives. This is important to understand. The structure of how people are remunerated is completely different in a private system. In a private system, costs are continually being squeezed — if they are not, then the owner of the business will make no profit. This is because in a competitive economy, other businesses will be cutting their costs and cutting their prices. If any individual business does not cut its prices, then all the consumers will buy from the ones that do cut their prices. Thus everyone is constantly trying to control their costs so that they can drop their prices in order that they will get more business, resulting in increased profitability.

Alternatively, the private company may try to supply more value for the same money. The process works in the same way. It is impossible to be complacent in such an environment! Companies must constantly strive to improve their service and lower their costs.

Government organisations are totally different — there are no such incentives to control costs. If a public company makes a loss, the government pays the loss. If the company makes a profit, the managers do not benefit. Not only is there the absence of a profit motive mechanism, there is the existence of another mechanism.

What happens is that the civil servant who has the biggest staff and the biggest budget is considered the most important and gets paid the biggest salary. Therefore, there is an incentive for a government employee to expand his/her budgets and increase costs to justify increasing the amount of money that should be spent. The process for getting this extra money is very different from the process of selling more products. Instead it is a process of going to government and justifying an additional amount of expenditure or an extra cost. If this cost becomes obsolete, there is no mechanism for cutting that cost, as there is nobody with an incentive to do so. Therefore, we can see that all departments in the public sector have an incentive to increase costs, while companies in the private sector have an incentive to decrease costs and improve service. This is why businesses run far better in the private sector than in the public sector. This is why ordinary people can save sizeable amounts if important services are run by the private sector. Knowledge of how this process works is the key to understanding the benefits of privatisation.

In his well-known and highly entertaining short book, Parkinson's Law, Northcote Parkinson reveals that in the laws of public organisations, "work expands to fill the time allotted to it... government departments expand to fill the degree of competence of the chief civil servant in extracting money from the centre." There is no profit motive and no price mechanism in government organisations. If the civil servant makes cost cuts he or she receives no profit from this.

Costs in government organisations tend to increase and levels of services decrease with time. What incentive does the civil servant have to serve customers? They are not going to pay more for good service or less for bad. If they move their business elsewhere, what does it matter? Proper procedure and an orderly manner are paramount, while customer service and innovation are unknowns. Why do we allow any of our national resources to be exposed to this system when they could be part of the vibrant private sector — constantly striving to improve service, cutting costs and thus prices, and bringing out new and better products?

Incentives apply to investment as well as consumption. One of the main reasons governments finally decide to privatise nationalised industries in that they need vast injections of capital after enduring under-investment — sometimes for decades. The reason for this is that in the private sector, businesses can see that if they invest now, they will increase their profits in the future. In the public sector, it is not worthwhile for anybody to sacrifice anything now. Even if the project is successful, the bureaucrat will not benefit, but will probably feel the consequences of the sacrifice. There are therefore no incentives to ensure the necessary amount of investment in public departments. If this is true in the developed world, how much more so in poorer countries? In order to provide adequate amounts of capital efficiently utilised, it is necessary to privatise education, health, telecommunications, policing, electricity and justice. If this does not take place, these industries may continue indefinitely, steadily declining.

Public Choice

We know now from the theory of public choice that governments are not benevolent guardians, but act according to their own interests. Politicians may not always act in the best interests of the country, but do what will get them votes. They will also usually do what is of short-term benefit — such as inflating the economy before the election, despite the well-known fact that the consequences of such actions bear costs that far outstrip the benefits. Increasing the borrowings of the government so that we must pay, with interest in the future, is another example of governments responding to interests that are not those of the individual. Since the democratic process is such a poor reflection of our wishes, we must turn instead to the market — which really is the best democracy. We vote every time we shop - prices reflect our opinions and desires most accurately and what we buy feeds back to producers who listen carefully to what we say.

Privatisation is not likely to come at the expense of your voice being heard but it will be heard in a different way, or rather in the way it has been best heard up till now: through the things you buy and sell. Few people's views are taken into account in the political process. It is simply impossible to consider every one of several million opinions, even if it is possible to know them. Even if it is possible it may not be desirable.

Rebels Without a Clue?

Information

It is especially true now, although it has always been true, that politicians (or anyone else) cannot understand the consequences of the decisions that they make. Good decisions are based on knowing the relevant information in each case. Government Acts basically impose one decision on thousands of different situations that would otherwise be resolved differently in each case. Armed only with statistical aggregates, it is impossible for governments to know even a small fraction of the information needed to make a good decision. The optimal decision would involve many different applications in hundreds of different circumstances for which it is impossible to legislate. Even if these problems were solvable — which they are not, such decisions would have to be reviewed on a weekly basis as conditions change to produce optimum results. The conclusion is that decisions should be left to the market where they will each be made by the thousands of individual decision-makers, who have the best information to make them, who can watch the consequence of their individual decisions and who can react accordingly.

Markets are not chaotic but highly ordered. They are not simply ordered by an outside third party (the state), but by the individual decisions of individuals who know what to do as a result of the price mechanism. The fact that they are unpredictable is because they are full of activity. When an industry is tied down by regulation it may seem more ordered and predicable but that is because little is happening.

While this applies to laws and regulations, taxes are similar. When governments raise taxes, spending these increases have unpredictable, but negative consequences, like large deficits, higher unemployment and benefit take-ups. Productive immigrants go elsewhere. The only thing that is predictable is that government economists will then appeal for higher tax rates. Governments are clearly not the best institutions to be making decisions about society.

The Price Mechanism

What prices do is widely misunderstood. Even people taken seriously as writers on economics can make statements like the following on the very first page of their book: "[prices] changed without regard for their effect on society" (Gray, 1998: 1). Actually, in a market prices change in line with the demands of society. That is what prices are! They are the result of the combination of the buying and selling decisions of everyone in society. They reflect your needs and mine far better than any voting process ever could.

Rebels Without a Clue?

The price mechanism is one of the most amazing features of a market economy. Whenever people buy more of a commodity, the price goes up and that tells suppliers to supply more and when people buy less, it goes down and that tells suppliers to supply less of that commodity and concentrate on something else. For the myriad of goods and services that we buy every year, the information expressed in the price tells suppliers exactly what the wants of society are. This is a simple, cheap and effective way of making sure people get what they want to buy and that the products that nobody wants are not supplied or produced. This should be contrasted with the armies of expensive planners and statisticians that governments need for a job of co-ordination that does not even begin to approach the simple efficiency and elegance of the price mechanism. Despite the expense of the planners, most communist industries produced goods that nobody wanted to buy.

If the state cannot understand the economy in the absence of the price mechanism, it is also unable to control itself. The state sector cannot be controlled in its size or its scope, and its inherent nature cannot be changed by the actions of government. Government leaders are not ceding as much power as they might think in privatising departments. They never really controlled what happened anyway. Bureaucracies decide for themselves what they will do, that is partly why they are so ineffective. Pertinent information and management talent are not available everywhere. For example, in Zambia where the decentralisation of public health is underway, there is a need for careful planning at a local level, but Zambia does not have that capacity. Full privatisation does not require that kind of "careful planning" since the price mechanism will ensure that resources are allocated where they are most needed. Price mechanisms are in fact, a planning method that works 100 times better than central planning for 1% of the cost!

In a Free Market, people choose what they want to buy, from whom they want to buy and for how much they want to buy a service or product. Some people may wish to have 20 pairs of shoes, others just 1. This ensures efficient use of resources. For example, if people want to buy leather shoes, a demand for leather shoes exists – then suppliers can meet the demand. If people do not want to buy leather shoes, but instead wishes to buy leather jackets, then the supply will have to change and the best use is made of the resource(leather).

However, in Socialism, the State decides what people want. And when people do not want what they are supposed to want, the State simply forces people to submit to the States whims. The State forces exchange and this causes the waste of many resources that could be used otherwise. For a more in depth discussion of this see Hayek (1944) Chapter 4.

Even socialists like Gray recognise the importance of the price mechanism in their better moments (1998: 136), like when describing why socialism/communism did not work in Russia. Inconsistently, they fail to apply the same model to why education, health, policing and other functions currently run by the state do not work and could do much better in private hands with a price mechanism and proper incentives. More on the Price Mechanism can be found at Friedman (1979: 14).

A Discovery Process

Markets are a process of discovery. Better ways of doing things would never have been discovered in some cases if there were no free market. This has dire consequences in the case of health and education, for example. If health and education were wholly private, then better ways of healing people and better ways of educating people would be discovered. In a free market situation there are strong incentives for owners to try out new things and for others to copy them. In government institutions any risk-taking is all cost and no benefit, so very little is ever discovered.

The state took over the provision of most services not because the private provision was problematic but to augment its own power or finances. Roads were started privately by tolling companies, taken over by the state later on. Education in the UK was private up to the 1870 act and by the time it was taken over by the state, the church and private schools had achieved virtually 100% literacy, an achievement that the state system has not achieved to this day. British hospitals were nationalized in the 1950s when they were functioning well, and since then there has been little investment or improvement compared to private sector achievements. The provision of policing was private up to the 1820s when Peel nationalised the provision of the service with results that were very disappointing compared to the hope of the proponents; crime has been continually increasing in many countries under public policing systems.

Even the provision of law which might be considered one of the most basic of government services was originally and better provided by the private sector. The merchant's law of medieval times was wholly developed by private agencies without the state and enforced its decrees by the fact that no one would trade with the merchant's. Merchant's law was superior to later royal law because it was quicker, less complicated and presumably cheaper, since the royal courts were basically income-producing devices for the crown. Law enforcement became public mostly because of the state's desire for more revenue. Since none of these areas are in the public sector for good reason, there is no good reason not to return them to the private sector where they can produce results consistent with the demands of the population

Rebels Without a Clue?

Free Market Planning

From Reisman:

> "And now, once more with credit to Mises, so far from being the planless chaos and "anarchy of production" that is alleged by Marxists, capitalism is in actuality as thoroughly and rationally planned an economic system as it is possible to have. (The lack of this understanding characterised Gray's analysis (Gray 1998 73-4). The planning that goes on under capitalism, without hardly ever being recognized as such, is the planning of *each individual participant* in the economic system. Every individual who thinks about a course of economic activity that would be of benefit to him and how to carry it out is engaged in economic planning. Individuals *plan* to buy homes, automobiles, appliances, and, indeed, even groceries. They *plan* what jobs to train for and where to offer and apply the abilities they possess. Business firms *plan* to introduce new products or discontinue existing products; they *plan* to change their methods of production or continue to use the methods they presently use; they *plan* to open branches or close branches; they *plan* to hire new workers or layoff workers they presently employ; they *plan* to add to their inventories or reduce their inventories.
>
> Still more examples of routine, everyday economic planning by private individuals and businesses could be found. Private economic planning is everywhere around us and everyone engages in it. However, to everyone except students of Mises, it is invisible. To those who are ignorant of Mises, economic planning is the province of government.
>
> Immense, all-pervasive private economic planning not only exists, but it is also all *coordinated, integrated, harmonized* to produce a cohesively planned economic system. The means by which this is accomplished is *the price system*. All of the economic planning of private individuals and business firms takes place based on a consideration of prices—prices constituting costs and prices constituting revenue or income. Individuals planning to buy goods or services of any kind always consider the prices of those goods and services and are prepared to change their plans in the face of price changes. Individuals planning to sell goods or services always consider the prices they can expect for their goods or services and are also prepared to change their plans in the face of price changes. Business firms, of course,

Rebels Without a Clue?

base their plans on a consideration both of sales revenues and of costs and thus of the respective prices constituting both, and are prepared to change their plans in response to changes in profitability.

Thus, for example, when my wife and I first moved to California, our housing plan was to purchase a house high on a hill overlooking the Pacific Ocean. However, after learning the price of such houses, we quickly decided that we needed to revise our housing plan and look for a house several miles inland instead. In this way, we were led to change our housing plan in a way that made it harmonize with the plans of other people, who also planned to buy the kind of house we were originally planning to buy but, in addition, were willing and able to commit to their plan more money than we were willing and able to commit. The higher bids of others and our consideration of those bids brought about a harmonization of our housing plan with theirs.

Similarly, a naive college freshman might have a career plan that calls for him to major in Medieval French literature or Renaissance poetry. However, sometime before the start of his junior year, he comes to realize that if he persists in such a career plan, he can expect to live his life starving in a garret. On the other hand, if he changes his career plan and majors in a field such as accounting or engineering, he can expect to live very comfortably. And so he changes his career plan and major. In changing his career plan on the basis of a consideration of prospective income, the student is making a change that better accords with the plans of others in the economic system. For execution of the plans of others requires the services of far more accountants and engineers than it does the services of literary experts.

A last example: consumers change their dietary plan, and thus plan, say, to eat more fish and chicken and less red meat. This results in a corresponding change in their pattern of buying and abstention from buying. Now, in order to maintain their profitability, supermarkets and restaurants must plan to change their offerings, namely, to increase the respective quantities of fish and chicken and fish and chicken entrees or sandwiches they supply, and decrease the quantities of red meat and red-meat entrees or sandwiches they supply. These plan changes, and corresponding purchase changes, on the part of supermarkets and restaurants result in further plan changes and purchase changes, on the part of their suppliers and on the part of their suppliers' suppliers, and so on, until the entire economic system has been sufficiently replanned to accord with the change in the plans and purchases of the consumers.

The price system and the consideration of cost and revenue that it entails on the part of all individuals leads to the economic system continually being replanned in response to changes in demand or supply in a way that maximizes gains and minimizes losses and ensures that each individual process of production is carried on in a way that is maximally conducive to production in the rest of the economic system.

For example, as the result of a decrease in the supply of crude oil, there will be a rise in the price of crude oil and of oil products. All individual buyers will consider the higher prices in relation to their own specific circumstances—in the case of consumers, their own needs and desires; in the case of business firms, their ability to pass along the increase to customers. And all of them will consider the alternatives to the use of oil or oil products available to them specifically. Thus, on the basis of his individual thinking and planning, each of the participants will reduce his demand for the items in a way that least impairs his well-being. And in this way, the thinking and planning of all participants in the economic system who use oil or oil products will enter into the determination of where and by how much the quantity of oil and oil products demanded decreases in response to a rise in their price. This is clearly an instance of responding to a loss of supply in a way that minimizes the loss. The reduction in supply will be accompanied by an equivalent reduction in its use in the least important of the employments for which the previously larger supply had been sufficient.

Ironically, while capitalism is an economic system that is thoroughly and rationally planned, and continuously replanned in response to changes in economic conditions, socialism, as Mises has shown, is incapable of rational economic planning. In destroying the price system and its foundations, namely, private ownership of the means of production, the profit motive, and competition, socialism destroys the intellectual division of labour that is essential to rational economic planning. It makes the impossible demand that the planning of the economic system be carried out as an indivisible whole in a single mind that only an omniscient deity could possess.

Rebels Without a Clue?

What socialism represents is so far from rational economic planning that it is actually the *prohibition* of rational economic planning. In the first instance, by its very nature, it is a prohibition of economic planning by everyone except the dictator and the other members of the central planning board. They are to enjoy a monopoly privilege on planning, in the absurd, virtually insane belief that their brains can achieve the all-seeing, all-knowing capabilities of omniscient deities. They cannot. Thus, what socialism actually represents is the attempt to substitute the thinking and planning of one man, or at most of a mere handful of men, for the thinking and planning of tens and hundreds of millions, indeed, of billions of men. By its nature, this attempt to make the brains of so few meet the needs of so many has no more prospect of success than would an attempt to make the legs of so few the vehicle for carrying the weight of so many.

To have rational economic planning, the independent thinking and planning of all are required, operating in an environment of private ownership of the means of production (including health, education etc) and the price system, i.e., capitalism."(Reismann 2002)

The Division of labour

"The division of labour, a leading feature of capitalism, which can exist in highly developed form only under capitalism, provides among other major benefits, the enormous gains from the multiplication of the amount of knowledge that enters into the productive process and its continuing, progressive increase. Just consider: each distinct occupation, each sub-occupation, has its own distinct body of knowledge. In a division-of-labour, capitalist society, there are as many distinct bodies of knowledge entering into the productive process as there are distinct jobs. The totality of this knowledge operates to the benefit of each individual, in his capacity as a consumer, when he buys the products produced by others—and much or most of it also in his capacity as a producer, insofar as his production is aided by the use of capital goods previously produced by others.

Thus a given individual may work as a carpenter, say. His specialized body of knowledge is that of carpentry. However, in his capacity as a consumer, he obtains the benefit of all the other distinct occupations throughout the economic system. The existence of such an extended body of knowledge is essential to the very existence of many products—all products that require in their production more knowledge than any one individual or small number of individuals can hold. Such products, of course, include machinery, which could simply not be produced in the absence of an extensive division of labour and the vast body of knowledge it represents.

Moreover, in a division-of- labour, capitalist society, a large proportion of the most intelligent and ambitious members of society, such as geniuses and other individuals of great ability, choose their concentrations precisely in areas that have the effect of progressively improving and increasing the volume of knowledge that is applied in production. This is the effect of such individuals concentrating on areas such as science, invention, and business." (Reisman, 2002)

Jane Jacobs in "Cities and the Wealth of Nations" goes into considerable depth on how this affects factories built in the middle of the desert by the governments of oil rich countries. The huge division of labour needed for the production of anything is thus revealed as the factory cannot function without the thousands of diverse component makers and suppliers existing in the places factories usually are sited. No one realises how many people are involved in making the simplest of components. One famous essay explores the thousands of people, skills and knowledge bases that go into making just one pencil. This is why government processes where the minister or permanent secretary is effectively being expected to know for their industry, be it education, policing, making pencils or running a hotel, all the millions of pieces of information necessary to provide a particular good or service is unrealistic. The task is, of course, impossible, which is why everything that government currently does must be returned to the private sector where it belongs.

The most famous example is of course, the pin factory that Adam Smith visited where he discovered the effectiveness of having different people maximizing the production of an individual part of the process.

Frank (2002: 189) points out that inside a corporation is an exercise in central planning. This is true to a degree and that is why (as he mentions) people are now trying to turn the internal workings of big corporations into something more like an internal market. However, there are two reasons why efficient corporate planning does not mean it can work for a country. The first is incentives: there is always a drive to do things better, faster or quicker because owners loose or gain based on performance. This does not happen in a government. The second thing is size, small companies can "central plan" because they are only dealing with a small situation. As Von Mises talks about at length, the free market is not
"no planning" – it is the coordination of millions of small plans (of ordinary people) rather than the one plan of an elite who cannot know or care about the needs of people that would have been expressed in their little plans if they had been allowed to express them.

Rebels Without a Clue?

The balance of control

. As people decide to buy or not to buy, the market adjusts and prices and uses of resources are balanced. This means that the captains of industry are the real heroes, the real servants of the people – they provide a way for people to decide their own lifestyles, their occupations and ultimately their destinies. For as people are free to buy and sell as they see fit, they gradually increase their standard of living. A historical example of this is the United States in the 19th and early 20th centuries – as Free Market principles were implemented, they became one of the wealthiest countries in history. In the words of George Reisman:

> "At least since the time of Adam Smith and David Ricardo, it has been known that there is a tendency in a capitalist economy toward an equalisation of the rate of profit, or rate of return, on capital across all branches of the economic system. Where rates of return are above average, they provide the incentive and the means for stepped up investment and thus more production and supply, which then operates to reduce prices and the rate of return. Where rates of return are below average, the result is reduced investment and reduced production and supply, followed by a rise in profits and the rate of return. Thus, high rates of profit come down and low rates come up.
>
> The operation of this principle not only serves to keep the different branches of a capitalist economy in a proper balance with one another, but it also serves to give the consumers the power to determine the relative size of the various industries, simply on the basis of their pattern of buying and abstention from buying, to use the words of von Mises. Where the consumers spend more, profits rise, and where they spend less, profits fall. In response to the higher profits, investment and production are increased, and in response to the lower profits or losses, they are decreased. Thus, the pattern of investment and production is made to follow the pattern of consumer spending.
>
> Perhaps even more importantly, the operation of the tendency toward a uniform rate of return on capital invested serves to bring about a pattern of progressive improvement in products and methods of production. Any given business can earn an above-average rate of return by introducing a new or improved product that consumers want to buy, or a more efficient, lower-cost method of producing an existing product. However, then the high profit it enjoys attracts competitors,

and once the innovation becomes generally adopted, the high profit disappears, with the result that the consumers gain the full benefit of the innovation. They end up getting better products and paying lower prices.

If the firm that made the innovation wants to continue to earn an exceptional rate of profit, it must introduce further innovations, which end up with the same results. Earning a high rate of profit for a prolonged period of time requires the introduction of a continuing *series* of innovations, with the consumers obtaining the full benefit of all of the innovations up to the most recent ones." (Reisman 2002)

The Profit Motive as the Foundation of Economic Improvement

What the intellectuals' hostility to profits and the profit motive ignores is that the quest for profit in a free market is the source of virtually all economic improvement. In a free market, what one is free of or from is physical force, including fraud. Since this principle applies to everyone, one is at the same time oneself prohibited from taking the property of others against their will, which includes taking it by dishonest means. Anything one receives from others must be by their voluntary choice.
In a free market, the way one obtains money from others is by offering them something they judge to be valuable and desire to have. These are the kinds of things one seeks to produce and sell. In this way, the profit motive is the foundation of the continuous introduction of new and improved products and methods of production. The development of new and improved products that people will want to buy, and the more efficient, lower-cost production of what they already want to buy, are the leading ways in which businessmen make profits in a free market.

No less ignored by today's intellectuals is the fact that the overwhelming bulk of profits in a free economy is saved and reinvested, and that the accumulation of any great fortune in a free economy is the result of introducing a whole series of improvements and using the far greater part of the resulting profits to create the means of delivering those improvements to the general public.

Thus, as a classic example, Henry Ford, who started with a capital of about $25,000 in 1903 and finished with a capital of about $1 billion at the time of his death in 1946, was responsible for a major part of the tremendous improvements made in the kinds of automobiles produced over that period and in the efficiency with which they were produced. It was largely thanks to him that the automobiles of 1946 were so far superior to those of 1903 and had declined in real cost from a point comparable to that of a yacht to a point where practically everyone could afford an automobile. At

Rebels Without a Clue?

the same time, Ford's growing fortune was invested precisely in the growing production of such improved automobiles. In other words, the other side of the coin of Ford's growing fortune was the general public's growing benefit.

A more recent and equally obvious example of the same principle is the case of Intel. In the early 1980s, Intel was in the forefront of producing what was then the most advanced chip for use in personal computers: the 8086. Competition did not allow the high profits it made from that chip to last very long, however. To continue earning a high rate of profit in the computer-chip industry, it was necessary for Intel to introduce the greatly improved 80286 chip. And then the same story repeated itself, and to continue earning a high rate of profit in the face of the competition always nipping at its heels, Intel had to develop and introduce the 80386, then the 80486, and then successive generations of the so-called Pentium chip. Intel has made a fortune in the process. Its fortune is invested precisely in the production of today's radically improved computer chips that are produced at a small fraction of the cost per megabyte of the chips of a decade or two ago. (Of course, the profits earned from any given improvement can often be invested in expanding the production of other, totally different products as well.)

These examples are not isolated. The principle they illustrate operates universally, to the extent that the market is free. Its greatest illustration can be seen in the whole rise in the standard of living that has taken place over the last 100 years. In 1902, the average worker worked about 60 hours a week. What he received in return was the average standard of living of 1902 - a standard of living that did not include such goods as automobiles, air conditioners, air travel, antibiotics, refrigerators, freezers, motion pictures, television sets, VCRs, DVD players, radios, phonographs, CD players, or personal computers. Telephones and electric light and power were uncommon. Electric appliances were virtually unheard of. Cell phones, of course, were entirely nonexistent. The goods that could be produced, such as various kinds of food, clothing, and shelter, were all far more expensive in real terms than they are today--that is, in terms of the time needed to earn the money required to buy them. The diet, wardrobe, and housing of the average person was far more modest then than now. These goods became more affordable and improved in quality and variety only as the quest for profits led to the necessary cost-cutting and other improvements in their production. And all of the goods that did not exist at all in 1902 came into existence only because of the quest for profits.

In other words, what so radically improved the standard of living of everyone was nothing other than the existence of the profit motive and the freedom to act on it as the guiding principle of production and economic activity. Everywhere, in every industry, in every town and city, there were men eager to profit by improving products and methods of production. They were free to do so, and they succeeded. This "greed," infectious to the point of being all-pervasive, is what so radically improved the standard of living of the average person. It is something we should all be profoundly grateful for. To whatever extent it would have been less "infectious" and less pervasive, the improvement in the standard of living would have been less.

The extent of the improvement for the average person can be gauged from the fact that his standard of living of today can be taken as at least 10 times that of 1902, and it is obtained by performing on average only two-thirds as much labour--40 hours of labour per week instead of 60. Thus, two-thirds the labour of 1902 now earns the money sufficient to buy 10 times the goods! A mere tenth of that two-thirds, or 6 2/3 percent, is today sufficient to buy goods equivalent to the average standard of living of 1902. This means that on average, thanks to the "greed" of businessmen and capitalists, there has been a fall in real prices since 1902 on the order of 93 1/3 percent! (Source: www.mises.org).

Ownership of Capital Is Widely Spread, Not Concentrated, In Modern Free Market Economies

For the most part, capital is owned by everyone in society through the ownership of shares, unit trusts, mutual funds, deposits at the bank, company pension funds and houses in a free market society. When we talk about capitalists in modern society, we are talking about ourselves. One of the theoretical definitions of the achievement of socialism is that it exists only when the means of production are owned by ordinary people. If this is the ideal, then we are already there, capitalism has achieved a socialist ideal, again! The reason this is important, is that socialist rhetoric makes a lot of the idea that, as a result of capitalism, wealth and ownership is becoming more and more concentrated in the few. The fact is that that's not what has happened with respect to ownership since Marx predicted it.

The Market Needs Property Rights to Work

As lawyers (and even Reich (2002: 235)) are keen to point out, the market does not exist in a vacuum. Without a legal order it is not a free market – it is no market at all. Property rights and their enforcement are fundamental to the free market and absolutely must be protected – as explained eloquently in recent books like "Noblest Triumph" and others.
Gray talks about the enclosure acts converting common property to private property. I think this is a legitimate function of the state. However, that does not mean we should have taxes and government provision of 40% of the economy. It does mean we should convert existing common property like rights in views, heritage, atmosphere etc. into private property so that these resources can be properly managed. It is interesting that Gray (1998) neglects to mention that it was the enclosures that

Rebels Without a Clue?

created farming efficient enough to set us for the first time in history in the direction of the prosperity we all enjoy.

Running Down Capital Makes Socialism an Inevitably Temporary Phenomenon

One of the myths of welfare states is that by simply transferring wealth from the rich to the poor, a nation can enjoy a high standard of living – even if no-one has to work. Sweden has been hailed as a model welfare state for the past 40 years, boasting free medical care, generous welfare, less working hours and subsidies for almost anything. However, Swedes also pay exorbitant taxes – "well worth the services they obtain from the state" is the common remark in defence of these high taxes.

Recent studies have also shown that the average Swede earns only 68% of what the standard American is earning, and that Swedish production has fallen rapidly relative to American productivity between 1980 and 1999. While straight salary comparisons can be deceiving, and Sweden's cities are generally cleaner and more attractive than many US cities, the important finding is that welfare states are not making their citizens wealthier.

Welfare states vilify production and concentrate mainly on distribution. This causes welfare states to cannibalise their capital in order to keep the system ticking. This is an extremely important point. Therefore, socialism can never be a permanent state for a country. A Socialistic State can only live off the wealth created by Capitalism for a few decades and then it will have consumed all its wealth and will have to return to Capitalism or break up. This is what happened in Eastern Europe in the late 80s; it is what happened to the France of Louis the 16th; it is what happened to Medieval Europe after the Black Death.

Wealth transfer by the State actually destroys wealth. Success is penalised in the attempt to distribute wealth. If enough people are penalised for success, less people are likely to become successful. If less wealth is created in an economy, the poor are the first to feel it – so welfare states actually damage the poor. Welfare states, by confiscating profits, also damage capital formation. For example, in the medical profession of welfare states, most medical professionals have no incentive to buy new and better equipment, since the equipment is expensive and even if they do not keep up to date technologically, the people have nowhere else to go. The welfare state has turned new capital into a liability. This deterioration of capital has forced many companies (such as Volvo) in European welfare states to move abroad where their profits are not confiscated as readily.

Fortunately, the Swedes started off with a relatively high standard of living before Socialism started eating away their capital. Other European welfare states such as Spain and Italy (also with exorbitant taxes) are much worse off. Unfortunately, many welfare state proponents see the welfare state as morally superior and egalitarian while they eat away the future well-being of their economies. Socialism is a parasite, it can only exist until it has killed its host then it either returns to capitalism or everyone starves!

Common Misconception: Is investing in human capital vs. IT and systems the issue? (Responding Reich 1997)

Socialists sometimes imply that the choice between the free market and socialism is one between "investing in people" and "keeping the markets happy." The first problem with this view is of course, that markets are actually people too. Every time every person in society, rich or poor, buys or sells anything, we are the market. The market is all of us.

The second problem is that in fact governments run "people" businesses as badly as they run everything else. Education in the US, for example, despite having huge funding per pupil compared to the rest of the world has much lower education outcomes than say Hong Kong, where the education is mostly private or even Hungary, only ten years out of communism. Therefore, if governments really believed in "investing in people" they would immediately privatise education so that the investment could be made better. The same argument applies to universities. Therefore, instead of fighting for more government funding, the focus should have been on privatising them so that that the vast international pool of capital could be tapped in order to turn US high school education into something worthy of the country. Many will agree that having a highly trained workforce is a key to growth in the 21st century. This is the reason successful countries of the 2010s will be privatising universities and schools – so that the best available means of social organisation (the market) will be driving education forward. Those that will fail in the 2010s will be those that keep their education run by the most ineffective system known to man – government ownership and control.

Perceived disturbances to Free Market theories.

Those arguing against the free market will cite various conditions such as market failures or "public" goods as reasons why the free market will not work. Here we examine the these arguments and explore the real answers to these problems

Despite market failures

Rebels Without a Clue?

The fact that the market fails from time to time to produce perfect results is not a reason for government intervention. Even if the market is less than perfect, the argument remains that government control is even more imperfect! Not all alleged market failures were such in reality. Externalities can be solved without government ownership, control or regulation of the resources in question. The difference between the effects of government as opposed to private control is even greater in the Third World.

This does not necessarily mean that capitalism and its proponents are perfect. The system does not work perfectly and there are no perfect people about. Managers fire profitable people from time to time, people do things that do not maximise profits and competition is not always perfect. However, it is the best system precisely because it factors in that people are not perfect. No other system gets people working so hard to serve each other's needs! It does not need to be perfect — it just needs to be better than the alternatives, which it clearly is.

This is particularly evident in the way that regulators come to create very strange and negative results in the areas they regulate. The reason for this is that when a regulatory organisation is initially designed, the purpose is clearly defined, but once the organisation has achieved its purpose it has to create problems for the regulators to solve else everybody's jobs are at risk. Thus there is every incentive for organisations not to solve the problems they have been created to solve. Why then are we so surprised that government organisations are so poor at solving problems?

Dealing with "Public Goods"

The definition of public goods are those that it is impossible to exclude people from, so therefore people say they must be provided by the state. Gray holds that law and order, environmental protection and national defence are in this category. However by creating extra property rights, it is possible to provide all these goods privately. Thus by creating by law a tradable right that encapsulates the value of a view apart from any other rights to the property (to exclude others from walking there) you negate the need for government regulation of this. (Shaw 2002 303)

Its also worthwhile saying that even if it was true that these goods would be under provided in a market, in the case of law and order and environmental protection they are certainly under provided by government also. Furthermore, the only element of public goods that is even theoretically better for provision by the state is the payment for the good. Government is not good at providing these goods. Policing, justice and roads are radically underprovided in most countries.

There is thus no reason for defence, police, justice or environmental departments run by the state. The public good argument says that difficulty in excluding non payers makes the good underprovided. The maximum theoretical role of the state would be to collect the extra money that wasn't already being paid and pay it to the private companies that were providing the services in these areas. Socialists have used public goods arguments to justify a lot of areas that are not remotely needed to be provided by the state.

We should note here that while there might theoretically be losses from public goods provision being less due to governments not being able to enforce their edicts in the future. The gain from the reduction in tyranny across the board (which we have put up with for so long) is vastly larger than any loss from smaller provision of public goods, if any genuinely are public, which is doubtful.

Turner argues that one should argue one's case from the grounds of disliking public goods as if there were no way to internalise them and also as if public goods were a high percentage of the economy still in the state sector. We could probably privatise another 90% of state spending bringing tax to GNP rates in the West to 3-5% of GDP without running into any public goods problems that could not be easily overcome. Public goods problems to be justify the state's involvement have to be so inefficient that the ordinary 30 to 70% difference between private and public organisation is overcome. We would not expect that to happen often.

For how to deal privately with the following public goods see dougieshaw.com/dts1.html for law and order, noise, clean air, environmental protection and dougieshaw.com/privatisingeverything.html for parks, public health and a wide range of other goods.

The need for Equilibrium?

Classical economists almost imply that the free market only works in equilibrium. Therefore, Socialists have seized this as if to show that if equilibrium does not apply perfectly then the free market will not work. However, other more rigorous schools of free market though such as the Austrian school (www.mises.org) do not rely on theories of equilibrium to show the superiority of the free market. Equilibrium makes nice maths (its main function is to make economics more "scientific") but there are hundreds of reasons for the free market that do not rely on equilibrium.

The Assumption of Rationality

It is charged that economics rests on the assumption that people know their own self-interest, which is in fact not the case. In reality, for the market to work the best this is not a necessary assumption. What *is* required is that people, on average, know what they want *better* than a distant state can know. This is obviously true.

Rebels Without a Clue?

Furthermore, fundamentally even if a man did not know his own interests best, he should still have the freedom to pursue what he perceived to be his interest as freedom is in itself a value (Rothbard, 1970: 206). In order that people learn from their mistakes and successes, it is necessary that people should have this freedom.

If the state decides for people, they will never learn. Intellectual capital will not grow. Using force (the state) to create someone's best interests will create resentment in addition to the result which is not in their interest anyway. It is much better to create incentives for the man to consult private experts. These incentives are created by a state that everyone knows is not going to intervene.

Lastly, if individuals do not know their own best interests then government has no legitimacy either, since these same individuals, who allegedly do not know their best interests, would not know them at the ballot box either (Rothbard,1970: 206), Related to this is the idea that government should intervene to correct people's immoral choice. The problem here is the same. Governments are usually less moral than individuals are and they have no incentives to be moral especially with other people's choice. Furthermore, it is a wrongful infringement of their freedom. Moreover in this case if the state should intervene to correct any moral failure there is no logical reason why it should not correct all moral failure.. -More fundamentally, can force (the state) really advance morality? If a man is forced to be moral, is he really being moral at all? Government deciding every moral choice for us is the stuff of Orwell. Lastly, if people are not to be trusted to be moral, how can they then be trusted to vote morally for those who will police their morality? -
More fundamentally, can force (the state) really advance morality? If a man is forced to be moral, is he really being moral at all? If a person loves only because someone threatens to kill him if he doesn't, is he truly loving? Further discussion on these points can be found at Rothbard (1970: 206-212).

Measurement Issues

Tuner makes interesting points about how to measure prosperity, most of which I would agree with. Firstly, growth of GDP/capita (total income of society divided by number of people) is a better measure of individual prosperity than total GDP growth that could be growing due to population growth from immigration or an increased birth rate. A caveat however is that the growth of the second leads to more military security (high GDP means more overall ability to buy weapons) and if GDP growth grows through immigration from poorer countries then raising the income of these people is a good thing socially.

Rebels Without a Clue?

Measuring prosperity by income per hours worked rather than by income in total is only better if people do not enjoy their work. If they do, then it does not apply so well. Therefore, even if most of US's greater prosperity over Europe is from more hours worked (30-40% more hours worked), it is still an advantage (US is 35% more prosperous than the EU or France even in 1996 (Turner,2001: 134). This would probably be much more so today! People in France are not permitted to express the preference to work longer hours due to regulation. That is definitely not a good thing!

On the other hand, it is not unfair to say that the new economy preference for contract workers (exacerbated by labour market regulations that make contract workers better in a distorting way) means that in the US there is hidden unemployment when contracts are not renewed and people work part time when they would prefer to work full time. This is an information problem and online recruitment markets should help to solve this in a way it cannot in rigid, old-fashioned regulated markets, such as in France.

Labour productivity (how much each worker produces) is higher in Europe than the US but this statistic is distorted by the former's higher unemployment. Not having its lowest 5% of workers employed makes Europe's employed look artificially productive. A higher number of unproductive people dilute America's productivity. Capital productivity (how much production for every unit of capital) is higher in the US (an index of 94 US to 75 in Germany) though more capital is employed in Germany and France, (172 and 149 respectively compared to 128). This simply could indicate that Europe has the potential to increase its productivity by employing its capital more intensely (night shifts, more hours worked etc). On the other hand, it could mean Europe, due to distorted government incentives, has invested in bad projects. At a higher level, this seems to have happened in Singapore. Hong Kong has achieved the same level of growth with much less capital because its investment decisions were left to the market whereas those in Singapore were distorted by government policies.

Turner correctly points out that capital productivity, labour productivity or their sum, Total Factor Productivity, should not be maximised at all costs. Having 10% of the workforce working on only very high return products and 90% unemployed would still produce very high levels of labour, capital and thus total factor productivity - these can only be guides. The key indicator is economic growth (GDP growth/capita).

The calculation of GDP statistics is a subject in itself. GDP values a product at the price people pay for it. Actually, people may value it much more than that. The price of a product in a free market is actually the lowest suppliers are willing to supply it for rather than the worth to the purchaser which could be considerably higher. GDP stats count state spending as value when the value of what the state does is probably multiples smaller than its actual cost. This means the prosperity of countries with a

Rebels Without a Clue?

large state sector are greatly overvalued compared to those with smaller state sectors. Since most state industries save at least 20-40% of their costs when privatised while providing higher levels of service, we could probably reduce the value of state activities by about a third to a half. True, but how does this relate to the fact that they are overvalued in relation to the others – for example – it gives us a more fair comparison. Moreover, some state activities actually destroy value rather than creating anything at all.

Other difficulties include the non inclusion in GDP stats of housework (since no-ones buys it explicitly) which means if two mothers go out to work to look after each other's children it will show up as two new salaries in the GDP stats (Turner, 2001: 126). The effect of including these points in the GDP stats would increase the difference in performance between the market and socialism rather than reduce it.

Common Misconception: Are High Incomes for executives a problem if they are based on results?

Socialists are always complaining about high pay for executives. I also have a problem with high pay for executives when they are not creating value but that is a corporate governance problem. Socialists, however, have a problem even when they are creating huge value for society as a whole in cheaper prices and better products. If a CEO of a major corporation, like Andrew Carnegie's steel company in the 1800s, produces drops in price of a commodity of over 50%, thus providing huge knock-on benefits to the economy and ordinary people, then the many millions he gets is nothing compared to the value he has created. In fact despite the seemingly high salaries, the percentage earned of the value created by executives is a lot less than that of most employees. In other words if he gave away his whole salary that would do a little good, but the value he is adding in the marketplace is much, much bigger than that.

A related issue is entertainers like Michael Jordan who get paid far more than the rest of the team. It is a "winner takes all" scenario (or at least "winner takes most"). However, there are several reasons why it is not necessarily a bad thing. First of all, even though he is only a little bit better than other members of the team, the fact that the gap is worth so much gives team members strong incentive to do their absolute best to close it, thus providing us with better sportsmen, entertainers and CEOs.

Secondly, from a moral point of view if someone creates huge value for people, as sportsmen and CEOs doubtless do, and others are prepared to pay them for that talent, then whether it is $1 million or $100 million it's between the CEO/sportswoman and their customers. It has nothing to do with us. There is certainly no case for government intervention. Free marketers celebrate the success of others, knowing their success helps us, rather than harms us.

This is not to say overvaluations do not take place from time to time. The recent US stock market bubble have caused a number of inflated salaries. The bubble existed because of governments allowing money supply to run out of control. In these situations the only way to stop irrationally high salaries without value being added is to privatise the control of the money supply so that these bubbles do not happen. In the words of von Mises, after 1929, the action of the government should have been to do "nothing, sooner".

The Inevitability of the Free Market

The top 1% of British taxpayers shoulder 17% of the total income tax burden. They pay 30% more than the bottom 50% of earners, who contribute just 13% of income tax payments. In the USA, the rich shoulder an even more exaggerated burden, with the top 1% paying 28% of the total income tax receipts in 1994. Tele-conferencing, the Internet, virtual offices and the rest of the information revolution is making it increasingly easy for that top 1% to leave the high tax jurisdictions and still run their businesses in the developed countries, or on the Internet without paying the extortionate taxes currently expected of them. Lawyers, doctors, financial experts and accountants, are already, and will increasingly, offer their services using communications technology while actually residing in another (cheaper) country. For example, legions of high-tech workers have in recent years moved from Massachusetts to New Hampshire due to the lower tax rates there. People simply are refusing to be stolen from, and I do not see how Turner aims to stop them! Only 1.6% of US high school drop outs move to another state each year while fully 4% of college graduates do. The top people are getting more and more mobile. Privatisation with its concomitant tax cuts is the only solution to this threat.

A key theme in Turner(2001: 3) is that countries can resist privatisation and deregulation in a globalised world without cost. When there are large numbers of investors with huge amounts of capital looking for the most profitable home, it is difficult to see how a socialist country could increase its share in this. It is most likely to lose greatly to newer, more privatised economies.
Gray, though equally socialist, is closer to the mark "Global capital markets ...make social democracy unviable. By social democracy I mean: debt financed full employment, a comprehensive welfare state, and egalitarian tax policies....many core policies of social democracy cannot be sustained in an open economy." (This includes he adds, in its current impracticality, the implementation of the theories of Rawls)

Rebels Without a Clue?

Gray (1998: 90) relates disapprovingly, the way the bond markets heroically disciplined probably the most legendary larcenous state, Sweden, from borrowing any more from its children and stealing so much from its people. The debt amount had risen from 44% of GDP in 1990 to 95% in 1995. This forced Sweden to make sensible spending cuts, though they could relieve the pain if they had been prepared to privatise education and roll back the welfare state and give the money back to people in tax cuts.

Reich complains about public officials having to spend tax dollars on new sports stadiums to the detriment of schools in order to make sports teams stay in the area. The problem here is that both sports stadiums and schools are funded by the state. If both were privately owned and there were no city taxes then that would mostly likely be enough to make teams stay! If not, then it would attract other business that would make up for lost jobs or the fans could voluntarily contract with the team to stay.

However it is in the realm of ideas that socialism is truly dead, and the free market truly inevitable. Not only is the world aware that the idea that "government can solve problems" died with the collapse of the Soviet Union, but even its only defenders have defected. In a fascinating account by Franks (2002: 347), he explains how the top writers (Martin Jacques, George Mulgan) and editor (Charles Leadbeater) of Marxism Today, were the key thinkers and founder respectively of the New Labour think tank *Demos*. What is ever more interesting is that what *Demos* is promoting is entrepreneurship and the promise of the new economy. This is a huge indicator of the change in thinking! Even in a place as socialist as the UK, the prime defenders of socialism have become promoters of free market ideas. What ever happened to entrepreneurs as "oppressors of the people?" If even the writers for Marxism Today have realised that business people and workers are in a mutually beneficial relationship, what excuse has any socialist to remain in that sorry state?

Chapter 4

Wealth, Poverty and Markets

The perpetuation of socialist ideas causes poverty

"What causes poverty is the widespread belief that wealth does. It is wrong to demonise the rich precisely because this idea incapacitates the poor from moving up" (Gilder: 1981). The idea that one person's gain is another person's loss is a fallacy. Every voluntary trade makes things better for both parties or it would not take place. You buy a pair of shoes because they are worth more to you than the money you spend. The shop prefers the money to the shoes. Everyone gains. The rich can only get rich by benefiting others much more. The process of one person prospering through trade cannot make another person poor. However, if those on the left propagate these ideas, then the poor will believe that it is impossible for them to rise up and decide rationally for themselves that it is not worthwhile to exert the effort. In many ways, the ideas of socialism with all its assumed moral virtues, serves mostly to keep poor people poor.

Gilder(1981) interviewed prisoners to test this idea. He found that they nearly all had the same theory of economic success. That all wealth comes from stealing, and that they were just unlucky. Therefore, in other words they are criminals because they believed the lies of socialism, both that stealing was legitimate and that they could not succeed in life by their own efforts. Intellectuals in universities can have equally destructive ideologies when they say that money can only be made by exploiting workers, by polluting the environment or selling shoddy goods for high prices. In promoting these ideas they are telling people that by taking responsibility and working hard, they cannot get ahead. Many people doubtless give up trying because of these lies (Gregorsky, 1998: 119)

The idea that the poor will be able to afford less than the rich in a capitalist society is advanced as a moral argument, but displays weaknesses in the economic area. In the free market, an individual's income grows faster than it would under socialism. The poor will be able to afford less than the rich, but because of the growth of the economy, they will be able to buy far more than they would have done if the country had stayed socialist, despite transfers to the poor. The free market system provides the fastest rise in income, which is better for the poor — not a system that transfers money from the rich and in so doing, restricts the growth of the total distributable income.

Rebels Without a Clue?

High growth caused by capitalism: the best way to help the poor

Studies undertaken during the 1970s in the USA showed that 80% of those with zero net worth escaped poverty in a few years; to be replaced with those too old, too young, or too beset with children to have a positive asset balance. The process is continually repeated. The poor are not a constant group; they are constantly changing. Most of the poor will move out of that category in a few years without any help from the government. Thus there is little justification for government intervention when most of the poor move out of poverty within a few years anyway. Being a poor student is not considered a social problem. We all realise that this is a temporary state - and are likely to earn more within a few years. This is in fact the situation for many of the poor people in society. It is a temporary state, not a long-term social problem.

The key concern then is that over time the average income of the poor is increasing. Research shows that when the economy in general is growing the fastest, the income of the poor grows the fastest. This is of course contrary to the socialist myth that over time the rich get richer and the poor get poorer. In fact it proves this myth to be the absolute propaganda that it has always been.

A huge study done by the World Bank and analysed in the Economist (2001: 1 23) shows that incomes of the poor have gone up 1 for 1 with incomes of the general population across the world going back 40 years in 80 countries. In other words it is a long term, global phenomena. In fact the correlation between the growth of incomes of the poor and of everyone else is close to 1. Correlations this high are virtually unheard of in the social sciences. Herrnstein (1994: 67) says they are usually consider good if they are higher than 0.2! It is thus a clear, indisputable result of economic growth that the poor get richer when there is economic growth. Socialists, having been proved wrong on economic efficiency, have been hanging onto a thin thread of justification in their claim their policies are better for the poor. We now know that that is not true either.

Socialism is far more dehumanizing than capitalism

The argument that capitalism is dehumanising, has also been put forth — that because people have to work in order to earn a living, they are being exploited by those who employ them and that people are being treated as objects in a process rather than as unique individuals. The problem with this argument is that in a socialist collective, people are still part of a productive process. They still have to work and it is difficult to prove that they will necessarily be treated better in the workplace. In socialism everyone is submerged in the group, while with capitalism, every individual is unique and free. It is clear to see that there is more likelihood of poor treatment as part of a socialist collective.

Do the poor really not pay much in the way of tax?

One of the lines with which socialism justifies its evil ways is by claiming that the rich must be taxed to pay for the poor. In reality, however in every country the poor end up being taxed as well and usually end up bearing more of the costs of big government than those at the top of free market societies. Partly this is in the form of obvious taxation. Poor people pay VAT and/or sales taxes on everything they buy and often income tax and social security taxes on everything they earn. These burdens fall proportionately harder on them and any lessening of the power and wealth of the state benefits them the most compared to their incomes.

However, even when the poor do not bear any obvious taxes as with the rural poor in Africa, they actually still pay a heavy price thanks to the rest of the economy being taxed. For example, whenever they buy kerosene fuel to light their lamps they are paying for the customs taxes paid to import it. When they ride in a taxi, they pay for the fuel tax that all vehicles have to pay when they buy fuel. They also usually pay customs duties on the import of the vehicle. Poor countries do not often make their own cars. When they buy food at the shops, they pay for these same transport costs, (especially outlying, rural area- one of the poorest groups. They also pay for the payroll taxes on every employee involved in the process. The man who drives the truck to bring the food to them pays income tax. The people who pack the food made locally are paying taxes and the company may pay corporation tax as well. Those who work in the shops or wholesale companies often pay income tax as well. All these taxes are added to the price that a poor person pays for every single thing they ever buy. And it makes a unspeakable difference to their standard of living.

In addition, even taxes paid by business are funds that are normally used in an economy for employing more people to expand the business, so taxes paid by the rich simply deny jobs for the poor, the one thing the poor need most.
So let us not pretend anymore that socialism is somehow soaking the rich and helping the poor. It never has because it never can. Anything the state gives to the poor; it takes away with the other hand. It cannot do anything else; it has no funds of its own. The truth is you cannot separate who pays taxes. Any taxes end up being a cost on everyone in society. That is why low or zero taxes are always the best strategy for the poor. That is why the poor in the more private societies leave poverty

faster than they do in socialist countries. That is why privatisation is so necessary for anyone who genuinely wants to help the poor.

The kind of logical problem that one encounters commonly when people do not understand this is exemplified in Hines (2000: 173). He proposes to stop taxing labour and start taxing resources, little comprehending, it seems, that if the poor have to buy more highly taxed resources with their now slightly less taxed wages they are in exactly the same position as before!

Minimising the need for Charity

In a badly structured society with people of bad character, charity is needed everywhere and is never enough. In a well-structured free market society, charity is enough because it is only for a very small percentage of situations. In a free market there is little, if any, unemployment so there is no charity needed here. For drug addicts and alcoholics who steal to feed their habit there is debt service – where people learn discipline by compulsory working for others. For those who hit temporary hard times, there are low interest loans. These are enforceable with the penalty being that the borrower must work if he cannot pay the loan. For widows there is usually her family, for orphans there are usually relatives. Where there are not, there are efficient private adoptions companies competing to serve families that cannot have children (and operating of course much more effectively than the current government agencies.)

Education, Housing, Universities, Libraries, Museums, the Arts and Health should be free market businesses and are thus would not normally in a privatised world be in need of charity. This frees up huge amounts of charity that through government failure has to be devoted to these areas. Help for the blind, the disabled, and the environment are formed into foundations, funded by privatisation proceeds. The programs themselves run efficiently by competing private businesses. Mostly the programs would aid people to work, not necessarily providing handouts. This then is still charity. Therefore by freeing up funds, charity is increasingly more effective as there are fewer and fewer areas where it is needed.

. Opening orphanages, unless on a massive scale, cannot hope to do more for the public than providing a good product and continuously improving it, unless of course, orphanage services is your business. A business then does not need to do anymore for the "public good" than make their product.

Private foundations not government welfare

Rebels Without a Clue?

Private Foundations administering welfare could operate in the following manner. Their constitutions would govern that the funds could only be used for projects to which people had also *voluntarily* contributed funds. Therefore, people would when they donated in effect "vote" for the kinds of projects that are deemed to be the best causes. This would mean the money could always be used for the best purposes and bureaucratic inertia would not be able to set in. In addition, because there would only be a limited amount of money available for good causes, a list of all projects currently funded by the foundations could be listed on the Internet so people could see where the money is being spent. This would provide a sort of competitive market for sorting which projects are really desirable and which are less desirable, ensuring that available funds are channelled into the best projects.

It would also be prudent that the constitutions of these entities ensures that they would not be able to help anyone without that person agreeing to help others in some way. Not only would this develop the self respect of those who were helped and help build character in those who needed character improvement but it would also increase the amount of good done with the amounts donated.

Areas currently served by municipal government welfare and charities include helping the elderly repair their homes, clothing grants for poor children, continence services, emergency housing for floods, emergency personal situations, advice on careers, energy use, helping groups likely to be victims of discrimination, increasing awareness about matters of importance, public health issues, spiritual matters (churches), free school meals, funerals for the poor, recycling and gardening help for the aged. National emergencies are an area that foundations would deal with but it would be advisable to make this a loan that would be reclaimed rather than a gift to encourage people to buy insurance.

The "Poor" in the West

Socialists in the West talk about people earning "little more than the minimum wage" which is $7 to $8 an hour in the US or about $1200 a month, this is about 40 times the average wage in Zambia. By global standard there are really a very small percentage of people who are poor in the West.

It's Not a Battle between Rich and Poor

The socialist illusion is that rich people are being taxed to fund the poor. Actually not so. Firstly, there are not enough rich people to fund the poor. Secondly, rich people will not live in countries with high tax rates as they are internationally mobile. Third, as a result, governments tax the poor to give back only a percentage to the poor. Therefore, it is not an option or a reality for the poor to feed off the rich. Instead the parasite is Government. Governments drain all the money out of the economy and from the poor and then waste most of it. If you privatised everything and gave the money back in the form of reduced taxes the poor would benefit substantially. Therefore, it is more a battle between the poor and the state than between rich and poor. It is government that has all the Poor's money.

Everyone, owners and non owners, benefits from capital and from inheritances

Again from Reisman:
"In a market economy the non-owners obtain the benefit of the means of production owned by other people. They obtain this benefit as and when they buy the products of those means of production. To get the benefit of General Motors' factories and their equipment, or the benefit of Exxon's oil fields, pipelines, and refineries, I do not have to be a stockholder or a bondholder in those firms. I merely have to be in a position to buy an automobile, or gasoline, or whatever, that they produce. It cannot be stressed too strongly that these progressive gains, and the generally rising living standards that they translate into, vitally depend on the capitalist institutions of private ownership of the means of production, the profit motive, and economic competition, and would not be possible without them. It is these that underlie motivated, effective individual initiative in raising the standard of living.

A corollary of the general benefit from private ownership of the means of production is *the general benefit from the institution of inheritance.* Not only heirs but also *non*heirs benefit from its existence. The nonheirs benefit because the institution of inheritance encourages saving and capital accumulation, to the extent that it leads people to accumulate and maintain capital for transmission to their heirs. The result of the existence of this extra accumulated capital is additional means of production for the market, and thus more and better products for everyone to buy. The effect of additional capital, of course, is also an additional demand for labour, and thus higher wage rates. The demand for labour, it should be realised, is a major means by which *all* privately owned means of production operate to the benefit of nonowners. Capital underlies the demand for labour as well as the supply of products." (Reisman: 2002)

Soaking the Rich Hurts the Poor

The majority of the wealthy spend relatively little in the way of personal consumption. The majority of their wealth is invested in the production – which is what makes countries operate — the factories, the office blocks and salaries of workers (Gilder: 1981). The rich perform a vital function in our economies — to invest, which is what they, as a broad class, actually do. No one else can perform this risk-bearing role in society. In bearing this role, they foster opportunities for those with less money.

Rebels Without a Clue?

High taxes do not redistribute income, as much as they redistribute taxpayers — from their home country to foreign ones, from the office to the golf course and from documented business to underground (Gilder, 1984: 135). In addition, higher tax rates do not necessarily increase revenues: A US reduction of tax rate from 73% to 25%, in the second half of the 20th Century increased taxes collected by more than 200% and decreased the share the rich pay from 63% to 27%. A similar situation occurred in the UK in the 1980's. This is in stark contrast to 1976 where revenues dropped after the 50% tax hike, while VAT income only rose 45% when the rate doubled. Therefore raising taxes may not even be effective in taking money from the rich. In fact, there comes a point when it is not worthwhile to go to work if taxes move beyond a certain point.

If the activities of the rich, productive capitalists did not greatly benefit the poor, why did the losses of a million investors in 1929, create a depression for everyone else? Clearly, if the rich lose, then factories close, loans are hard to come by, job-creating investment slows and everyone loses out. There is a harmony of interests, what is good for the rich is also good for the poor and vice versa.

Businesspeople take great risks for the chance of being rich. More than two out of three new businesses collapse within the first five years. Although business failures are capitalised in new business knowledge, this does not help the entrepreneur who has risked everything and lost. Capitalists should be encouraged in the form of incentives, rather than penalised. Job creation is not without its possible costs to the entrepreneur.

The poor and the rich are constantly changing groups

Contrary to popular belief, like the poor, the rich are not a constant group. Of those with more than $60,000 in 1969, 85% had emerged in that generation. Few people who inherit large estates keep the wealth for another generation. This is in clear contradiction of the argument, put forward by Turner (2001: 240) that without redistribution the rich will get richer and the poor poorer with each successive generation. The children of the rich do not usually have the self discipline to sustain it, so permanent classes do not develop under capitalism.

Rebels Without a Clue?

Common Misconception: is inflation control an alternative to helping the poor?

Robert Reich argues in "Locked in the Cabinet" that Rubin's insistence of keeping rates high to "keep markets happy" is against the interests of the poor since as they are not lenders, they are not detrimentally affected. This is typical of socialism in its inability to fully think through the effects of policies. (Other examples would be the misunderstanding of minimum wage laws which price poor, unskilled people out of the market or rent controls that create a shortage of housing.) In this case, the poor may not be lenders but they are borrowers. If lenders are finding their loan portfolio's real value eroded by inflation, they will put up their rates, or alternatively stop lending altogether, hurting the poor. Furthermore, easy money policies cause wrong allocations of resources, which cause companies to loose money long term thus having less capacity to provide jobs for the poor.

Markets are disturbed when such things detrimentally affect the economy and thus the profits of companies. . If companies suffer there are no jobs for the poor. Keeping markets happy is therefore a good thing for the poor as they provide employment for the poor if governments don't drive them out of business through tax and regulation

Common Misconception: Does capitalism only listen to the rich? (Anderson 2002)

Welfare states are founded on such premises as:

- Free Markets not regulated by the state concentrate wealth in the hands of a few individuals, while most people become poorer
- The only solution is for the state to take from the rich and give to the poor
- This distribution of wealth causes the economy to grow, since more people will have more money to spend

However, history shows that in a Free Market system, individuals do not get rich unless they produce goods demanded by large numbers of people across all socioeconomic strata– for example, Henry Ford got rich by producing affordable cars, while manufacturers of expensive luxury cars at the same time did not show nearly as much profits. Similarly, Wal-Mart, by making many small convenience stores, has outdone Kmart that only offers fewer larger stores.

Therefore, only when consumers are purchasing on a large scale can producers, as a class, get rich. A few can individually serve richer niche markets, with the same effects. The theory of exchange – that economic exchanges produce mutual benefit – means that when the poor buy from the rich, no transfer of wealth occurs. Both parties win. In other words, the poor benefit from the transaction too – if both parties did not benefit, no transaction would take place. There is no exploitation! Thus the

Rebels Without a Clue?

Marxist premise that the rich only get richer if the poor get poorer is a flawed argument. So capitalism, being freedom orientated, is a method that helps everyone in society from the richest to the poorest with constantly improving products and constantly falling prices.

The Industrial Revolution : Good for the poor

One of the most popular myths perpetuated about the nineteenth century is that it was a time of hardship for the poorer half of society worse than anything that had gone before. This is patently untrue. Like in all previous centuries, the standard of living was lower than that of people today. In terms of the Nineteenth century, we can unequivocally say that by the end of the period the poorer half of the population where far better off than they were at the beginning. In order to achieve a greater effect, novelists (not historians) such as Dickens and Browning highlighted the extremes, in much the same way as TV stations do today.

In reality between 1842 and 1892 the number of paupers obtaining poor relief halved from 6.3% to only 2.6%. To put it even more starkly, the factory system offered a livelihood for tens of 1000s of youths who, under the pre-capitalist system would not even have lived to see adulthood. The pre-factory system, where the workers had a loom in their house, was far from ideal. The family paid heavily for the loom and took a big risk. If it did not work out, they would have had heavy debts. The average worker's house was damp and badly lit, and his diet poor.

The industrial revolution made the workers home more sanitary by removing the factory from it. "With singular unanimity in any country where they had the chance the poor have walked off the land into factories as fast as the factories could take them" (Rand: 1946). In addition the advantages of factories over agricultural work are quite significant: you get to working indoors rather than spending all day outside in the pouring rain or driving sleet (a particular advantage in Britain!), there is less physically hard work in the factories and there is the security of a wage rather than an uncertain harvest. Furthermore, wages were more generous with urban wages rising 43% during the period 1790-1831, while the cost of living only rose 11%.

The idea of children working in the factories is a strange one to the modern mind. However one has to bear in mind that up to that time children had always worked for the simple reason that in many families everyone's labour was needed just to keep bread on the table. It is only because of the economic growth that has come from the industrial revolution that we can now afford *not* to have children working. At the time that wasn't a realistic option. It is a common error to assume the people in times past had the money to do what we now have the money to do after a hundred years of economic growth (which we of course owe to capitalism). Moreover, it was the state

Rebels Without a Clue?

that put orphan children in the factories to learn a trade confirming that this was a view that was widely held, not just that of the factory owners. Apart from anything else families had always worked together in the fields or in the home factories and wanted to continue to do so.

"In France the quality and quantity of the peasants food grew rapidly from 1840" (Ascendancy of Europe 139). Consumption of both sugar and wine more than doubled from 1840 to 1880. Initial moves from cottage to factory brought sharp rises in cash wages and also in real wages. Coal and soap became cheaper and more plentiful, production of cotton clothes 1785-1840 increased ten times. In the 1840s workers could even afford carpets and comfortable furniture . "In France, the price of a quintal of wheat fell in 1850, for the first time in the country's history, to the equivalent of less than 100 hours of a labourer's work ... the British per capita consumption of tea, for example, trebled in 1844-76, and in the same years that of sugar increased from about 17 to about 60 pounds per head per year. .... every woman used to wear a blue or black dress that she kept for ten years without washing, for fear it might tear to pieces. However, now her husband, a poor worker, covers her with a robe of flowers for the price of a day's labour .... It became unnecessary for the poor to dress, as they had largely done hitherto, in the cast-off of the more well-to-do. " (Ascendancy of Europe 139-141)

Hours of work fell quite sharply in the latter decades of the nineteenth century and the early years of the twentieth. In Germany for example, the working year in mining and factory industries fell during the period of 1850-1913 by about 30%, while the working year for the employed population in general fell by about half as much. This improvement in consumption and conditions of work for the working-class in general, visible from the later decades of the nineteenth century, probably owed little to the activities of trade unions.

People often do not usually consider that mass production was for the masses! The purchasing power of the poor family increased by a factor of four during the course of the century – a huge increase that had never happened before. All thanks to that great friend of the poor, the free market system. The poor now had gas lighting and a wide range of cheap, reliable goods. The reality of starving people had always been present, but until modern times, the resources to change this were not available. The industrialisation brought about in this period produced a large drop in the amount of poverty the world experienced. Even the talk of the "growing middle class" means workers were becoming richer!

Rebels Without a Clue?

Labour laws: damaging the poor out of compassion for them

Reich spends the first 80% of his books explaining why labour laws, minimum wages, restrictions on hours, and so on do not work in the new economy and then unbelievably returns to them for a proposals for a minimum "decent" wage at the end (2002 243). Therefore, once again let us explain why these things do not work: a minimum wage by forbidding employers from contracting with willing employees below a certain rate ensures that the very poorest who have no skills are unemployable and never get a start, thus locking them into poverty. Therefore, socialism is horrible to the poor, always. It is a completely hypocritical ideology. Furthermore, by holding wages at a level greater than the value added by the person they give these people incentives not to train and become better.

In the future, "labour law" provisions can all be provided voluntarily on Internet listed employment contracts. Companies can provide opt outs from sickness benefits, maternity and paternity pay, and can provide ways for workers to choose the quality of their working environments versus more pay. There is no reason to force all workers to takes benefits (which in a competitive market ultimately come off their wages or are added to the prices they pay) when they might actually sometimes prefer more money in their pockets to spend. Alternatively, they may prefer nicer offices, but these are not choices that should be made for them by the government. Internet processes can make all these choices much more explicit and much more flexible.

All kinds of state regulation fit this paradigm. Allowing consumers to choose what regulations they want by making it easy to find out at the point of purchase what private quality standards a producer is certified for allows consumers to project the kind of choices Turner talks about (2001 187+) but in a much more effective way. Community Insurance (Reich 243) again is not a bad idea so long as it is done privately. If a region looses more than say, 5% of its economic base then the insurance will pay out to everyone. Alternatively, perhaps only those that have lost their jobs or perhaps only in such as way as to pay for new industry to come). It is not a bad smoothing mechanism. It would be cheap if many people contributed.

In terms of his suggestion for protection from trade, we should be aware that if this is paid to, and the premium is paid by, the industry affected then its fine. If government pays it then it is a form of protectionism and will prevent industry form adjusting to world trends and just make the problem worse in the end. Protecting industry never works.

As for what he says about kindergarten education, its fine, but it must be private. Its not government's role to provide these things. The whole point about the new economy is that government has to be minimal for you to succeed. You certainly should not impose it by force on people, which is what government provision is all about in reality. It is wrong. When he then talks about further taxes on high net worth citizen to fund schools you see that he has completely missed the point of his whole research project. Redistribution will simply move your high net worth people overseas. The only way to significantly improve schools for everyone is to privatise them.

Rising Welfarism and State Involvement

Much of the minimal but increasing state involvement in the nineteenth century is hailed today as a good thing. With a century of evidence behind us however we now know that state ownership and control are almost always negative in their impact and take away value and growth from economies.
Much of the state activity was wholly unnecessary because the private sector was already doing it before the state took it over. Unemployment insurance was provided initially by trade unions and then nationalized later. Education was growing very quickly when the state gradually started to get involved in Britain. Without state involvement these areas would have grown quicker than they did and education would have been provided that was better and cheaper than that which did in fact result.
The workhouse system (introduced by the Peel act of 1722) which ensured state help was the last resort helped achieve the above objective to some degree but the developing self insurance was far better. Having a poor rate at has the familiar effects of making it not worthwhile for the less skilled to work at all.
The 1792 change to the act removed the workhouse test giving people more on the dole than they would get working. Expenditure in 1818 reached 7.8 mil which is a huge 13s 4d /capita. In some places the poor rate reached 20s in the £ and farms were abandoned, landlords farmers and labourers were involved in common ruin. Whenever government, local or central, pays out money in welfare, it has to destroy jobs by taxing elsewhere. Moving money around the system does not solve the problem. If there is no state action what happens is that if there is unemployment then wages fall till everyone is employed again. And if the population is aware there will be no state action then they will buy unemployment insurance as many people did in the nineteenth century.
Glasgow and Edinburgh's local authorities had cleared unsanitary areas and installed new houses for the poor. A worthy act? Not really! In order to do so these local authorities would have had to levy taxes that destroyed jobs, productivity and good projects elsewhere. If the cities hadn't acted then just as gas and electrify and insurance were provided by joint stock companies so too would housing, water and sewage. The private system provides the maximum amount of goods to the poor and the rich for the minimum price. Waterlow had done the same type of project as a

wealthy individual; there were many ways to see cities developing without the need for state action.
A Public Health Act of 1875 forbade the building of new houses unless they had running water and internal drainage. Consider the effect of this on the lower classes who had enough money to buy a better house but not for one with running water and drainage. They wish to improve their accommodation and perhaps later move into a fully plumbed one if their situation improved in perhaps 10 years or so. Here we find they are unable to buy the property they want since builders are not allowed to build one. Alternatively they might like to buy the property now and add the drainage later on. By making certain classes of transactions illegal the Act here clearly diminishes the welfare of the very people that need their help. It is very rare for legislative action to improve things by more than they would have improved anyway. If people wanted drainage in their house (as they certainly did) then houses would have been increasingly provided with it as builders responded to demand. However, those who couldn't afford it at that particular time or for whom other housing factors were more important should not by force of law be force to buy something they do not want.
Industrial accident policies follow the same pattern. By 1911, when Switzerland introduced one, every advanced country in Europe had some form of state compensation for industrial accidents. By 1913, when the Netherlands introduced one, all had some kind of state insurance against sickness though this was often narrowly limited in scope and in some important cases, notably France and Italy, purely voluntary and not compulsory. Where the insurance was voluntary then there is no reason why an inefficient non-commercial organ like the state should provide when business could do so more efficiently. Where the insurance was compulsory we need to ask why people who perceive their risks to be low should be forced to pay for insurance that they do not consider suitable.
Roads were originally the responsibility of the parish. However, in the first half of the 18th century turnpike trusts (private enterprises) had been formed to look after the roads. By 1840 there were more than 1100 trusts which looked after 37,000 kms of highway. Roads were privately run originally. As usual, the state took over something already operational; they did not set up something the market wasn't providing. Notably many breakthroughs in roads appeared where they were privately run and curiously enough as with many other industries, when it were taken over by the state innovations and breakthroughs seemed to dry up
The population rose from 11 to 15 million from 1815 to 1835. Along with industrialism this led to a rise in urban housing needs that created conditions appalling by modern standards. However, we must bear in mind that, for the most part, people moved to the cities freely because they preferred the higher wages and opportunities of the cities to the equally long hours and hard physical work of farm life. At least factories kept you out of the rain!
The 1882 Electric Lighting act in Britain encouraged local authorities to provide lighting. The effect was to seriously limit private enterprise and put Britain "Twenty

years behind every other civilized country in the provision of commercial electricity". An apt illustration of the evil that frequently results from well intentioned legislation. Another hijacked invention was the telegraph again invented in the private sector it was developed in 1843 in Germany but unfortunately nationalized in 1868. The encroachment of state power into areas in which they had no business in which has been the hallmark of the 20th century was present in the seed form in the 19th century and unfortunately no religious or political leaders seemed to have the necessary ideological infrastructure to understand its destructive power.

Notice that nobody forced the workers to work 15 hour days and there were often many factories and other occupations available. Workers worked 15 hours because they preferred the extra money to the leisure time. Workers were hostile in Germany to the hour restricting laws correctly seeing these laws as restricting their incomes. Shop workers worked even longer hours: about 90 / week and bills in the UK to restrict this failed. These jobs were lower paid than factory jobs but women sometimes preferred the greater respectability of shop work. The key principle is that people should be free to choose their own hours of work. The government does not help anyone by restricting their freedom.

The state can rarely succeed in achieving economic goals. Peel tried a public works program in Ireland; as a result the other industries were starved of labour. It is very unusual in history for this type of program to solve more problems than it causes. Therefore, in summary we can see that the free market reforms of the late 18th and 19th century produced in the agricultural and industrial revolution a huge increase in the welfare of the poor. In contrast everything the state did by way of intervention could have done nothing but harm to the poor they were trying to help.

Unemployment in the Modern World

Unemployment is of course caused by unions or governments keeping wages above the free market level so that the poorer skilled people cannot be employed without losses. (Rothbard 1970 205)

Employment will be much more easily increased in service sectors than manufacturing. Indeed if welfare was abolished, the vast majority of people would find work in this sector. It adds to the value of your product to have more staff in a service-orientated business (i.e. more people behind the bar, more people answering phones, etc). On the other hand, more people in a factory nowadays are difficult to use because the process is automated. This was the experience of the "New Deal" in Britain. (Turner 2001 90,90n)

Involuntary unemployment is the measure to watch rather than employment rates as such since some of that may be due to individuals retiring early or just deciding to work less for less money and do other things instead. (Turner 2001 115) Involuntary unemployment includes where over 50s have decided not to bother due to low probability of finding work and women finding hour rigidity a barrier. These are all things an online system could deal with.

Rebels Without a Clue?

While the previous estimate of Europe's unemployment being 80-90% structural may be high, even if its 60 or 70% it is still a huge unnecessary cost to the very poorest in society. Even Turner admits (2001 153) that the situation is mostly caused by rigid labour markets when he observes the differences within Europe in rates (e.g. 2.5% in the Netherlands vs. 10% in otherwise similar Belgium) points to structural (i.e. government policy created) problems. Here is another clear example of where the more free market model is much better for the poor and the socialist model worse.

Connected with unemployment is the criticism of business (Frank 2000 191) every time workers are laid off, as if workers had a divine right to work there. The more important error though is the implication that left to themselves, without state intervention, companies would get rid of all their workers! The implication in the criticism is that companies employ workers out of a social conscience.
In reality of course, companies employ more workers to make more money so it is usual for them to keep their workers and it is usually profitable for them to do so.

When they lay off workers, it is because the workers have become unprofitable (i.e. they are subtracting rather than adding value to the rest of the people in the country). This can be self-induced (through unions) or simply through improvements in processes that make it possible to do more with less people. That gradual improvement of things is what over time makes everyone richer.

The important process to grasp, however, is that when goods and services are made cheaper because a company can do it with less money, the previous buyers of these goods then spend their savings elsewhere which creates jobs in the rest of the economy. Therefore, layoffs in the end create more work elsewhere. Furthermore, it is fundamentally good for everyone if less people are now needed to serve people in a particular way. This means these people can serve people in new ways creating more value in society i.e. a richer society.

Business: the big bad wolf?
In many books written by those of the "rebel without a clue" fraternity (e.g. Hines 2000) corporations and especially Trans National Corporations (aka Multinationals) are considered the source of all evil. What is entirely missed, usually, is firstly that with profit rates at around 5% of turnover most of the value of what these people do goes to customers and employees (who receive on average 80% of turnover.) Secondly, but as a corollary, if the demands of those that want to put more taxes and costly regulations are realised, in a competitive economy, the only result of this is to

increase prices to customers! Taxes on producers are ultimately taxes on consumers, including the poorest amongst them.
For a more in depth understand of how regulations cost consumers and free markets protect them see Friedman (1979 189+) which is Chapter 7 of "Free to Choose" entitled "Who Protects the Consumer."
The Welfare State did not work as expected.
In some ways, we were conned into accepting the welfare state by false promises. Beveridge (architect of the UK welfare state) told us that state spending (thus tax) on health would not rise because a healthier population would make fewer demands on the service. Yet spending rose relentlessly. (Micklethwait 2000 88)
More problems in practise of welfare states can be found in Friedman (1979 100+)

In other ways, it is just inappropriate for today's world.
When the pension age of 65 was set, people died on average at 45! Now they die at 76. Therefore, it is not feasible either for the relatively poorer youth to support a relatively richer elderly when most of the latter are quite capable of working and indeed have an enormous amount to give if they were not forcible retired or given incentives to stop contributing. (Micklethwait 2000 88)
In another sense, we are paying the price for having important institutions in the public sector. It is well know that those working for government organisations tend to vote for Statism, i.e. they vote left wing. This is because they view this as a way to higher salaries for themselves. It is also because almost by definition, if you work for the government you do not understand business and economics. You do not have to satisfy customers or go out of business. The problem with that is that in the case of schools and universities it actually creates an intellectual distortion of the facts. Statism affects the thinking of our best academics and thinking. Once schools and universities are privatised, the thinking of our best minds will be much clearer. In the knowledge economy, this is a necessity not a luxury.

What Marxism said would happen did not happen.
Marxism said over the century after he wrote that everyone would get poorer except the rich. In fact, capitalism produced the largest increase in the welfare of whole societies that had ever happened in history. Its time to put to rest the myth that capitalism in the long term ever makes the poor poorer.
Marx said revolution, in other words destruction and chaos would be the means of emancipation for the poor. It has not been.
Marx saw private property as a source of alienation for labour (North 1989 40) but we now know that societies with weak property rights remain in poverty the longest (De Soto 2000)

Problems with Democracy

Rebels Without a Clue?

Some people talk as if the voice of the people is the voice of God. It is not necessarily the case that the right thing to do is what the majority want. Often they have no clue about the economic issues. Furthermore, democracy brought us Hitler and Mussolini; it brought us the Sudanese government which went to anarchy then brutality. India is certainly a democracy but it its democracy has not brought its people out of poverty. Singapore has been a lot less democratic in its development, but it has been much more successful at getting rid of poverty.

When borrowers and lenders have different levels of representation in democracy, the latter can lead to institutionalized theft, a common feature of governments through the ages. For example, one of the first actions of the governments of the US after the revolution was to cancel the actions of the courts to enforce debts.

The central bank/ government coalition continually inflates the currency mostly because there are more borrowers than lenders and they do not like high interest rates. Artificially low interest rates however create booms and slumps that do more damage in the long run but democracy is responsible for these kinds of distortion. Democracy is a system where ordinary people vote collectively for a system to be imposed on everyone and are expensively taxed to provide it. The Market is a system where ordinary people decide each one for whatever they wish in terms of education, health, roads, food, cars, etc. It is a far better system.

So we can agree with Gray's second point in his summary, that democracy and the free market are competitors and firmly place our flag in the latter camp. (Gray 1998 213) (Frank 2000 15)

Frank is so obsessed with whether people agree with the policies or not that he spends most of the first 50 pages of his book discussing whether or not capitalism is or has been popular. That's not what's important. What's important is that it delivers the goods.

Chapter 5

Where We Are And Where We Are Going

Common Misconception: Have we already gone to some radically privatised extreme?

The state still controls 40% of GDP in most countries or more. When that gets to 1% or 2% we will have got to an extreme and will be far the more prosperous for it! It is of course possible as we have been there before. Government spent less than 10% of people's hard earned cash in 1900 and in the US it was only 3%.

Turner while clearly understanding many of the benefits of privatisation in Britain and elsewhere has a blind spot when he thinks Britain has nothing left to privatise. The same arguments he uses for all the entities privatised so far, apply even more to education, health, policing, justice, roads etc. as I have explained in depth in "Privatisation for Prosperity".(Shaw 2003).When he argues that the British are underskilled, privatisation of schools is the obvious solution based on his own arguments on privatisation (Turner 2001 218)

If we are to listen to Frank (2000) or other critics of the free market and his tales of how comprehensively free market thinking has swept America we might expect that the state has now shrunk to miniscule proportions.
As, *The Economist*'s book on Globalisation (Economist 2001 27) puts it "not as quickly as one might wish." (The article examines the issue in more depth and can also be found on their website (www.economist.com))
Unfortunately, for all the talk, the state is still about the same size as it ever was.

Common Misconception: Should balance be sought between Capitalism and Socialism?

People should not look for a balance with socialism any more than they should look for a balance with racism or genocide. Therefore, socialism is an evil, it should be avoided entirely. If we know that businesses operating competitively produce better and cheaper products and services than government owned enterprises, then why would we want anything run by the less efficient method? Why, especially, would be want really important things like education, health, policing and justice run by such a dreadful system? The fact that these things are normally in the public sector is a

Rebels Without a Clue?

remnant from a time when people and economists genuinely thought that socialism and government ownership was a better and more efficient way of producing goods and services. Yep, less than 30 years ago, a lot of intelligent people genuinely believed that. Amazing but true!

Very few people now believe that in general services are more efficiently provided by the government sector. Therefore, all goods currently provided by the government should be privatised.

This means half measures like Build Own Operate, Contacting Out, Private Finance initiatives should be avoided. It must be fully privatised to get the majority of the benefits with no monopolies and with competition instead of regulation. Resisting PFI is one of the (very) few points on which I agree with Hines (2000 177) where he (and the Lancet) argue that PFI simply moves the asset off the governments balance sheet, and I would add without the resource allocation benefits of a fully privatised health service, especially for the poor.

Hayek (1944 31) argues that trying to combine aspects of central planning and free markets creates a system that is worse than both. For a fuller discussion of why, this would be the book to read. Rand (1946: 144+, 183+) discusses how serious a mistake it is to regard compromise in what is basically a battle between good and evil, as having any place. The Free market in every sector is where we want to get to, not a bit of capitalism and a bit of socialism. That is suicide.

Nowadays, socialists argue on grounds of subsidising the poor since their greater efficiency argument of thirty years ago has proved false. Their current argument is however no better. There is no need to have anything in the public sector in order to subsidise it. Schools, hospitals and courts could all be efficiently run by the private sector and the poorest segment could still be subsidised. Therefore, an ostensible concern for the poor is no reason to keep things in the public sector. In fact, it is a reason to privatise for two reasons, firstly the poor will benefit from the lower cost that privatisation brings (so long as monopolies are not granted and expensive regulations are not imposed) and secondly, the tax cuts that come from the government no longer providing will bring down the overall price of goods and services which will disproportionately help the poor.

Contrary to popular belief, the free market is much better for the poor than socialism. Connected to the last Common Misconception is another: "People that promote the free market are ideological, worship markets, and are inflexible"

The overwhelming evidence, now little doubted even by those that write against free markets and globalisation (Turner 2001 8), is that the market mechanism is much better than a state mechanism at achieving objectives. Those who stick to what works rigorously and object to socialism most consistently are the ones who will be most likely to do the most good. Mixing a good approach with a bad one is not really a good technique. The more people are committed to the free market, the more we should listen to them. Caricaturing those consistently promoting the best system as "worshipping markets", or ideological or whatever, is wrong as it may deter the promotion of the best system going into operation in that country or context.

Rebels Without a Clue?

Common Misconception: are nation states really not obsolete?

Ohmae, famously, in "The End of the Nation State" argues that in a new globalised world, nation states will fade away. Gray disagrees saying that they will continue but his argument is not persuasive (Gray 1998 76). While he quotes Negroponte " Like a mothball which goes from solid to gas directly, I expect the nation state to evaporate" (Gray 1998 68) he does not seem to grasp why. The point is, and this is also what I expect to happen, Nation States can survive only until a few countries start to dispense with them. Then, since these countries will get all the investment, the process will accelerate extremely rapidly from that point. Therefore, it is not a gradual process but more like breaching a dam. We are not suggesting the state should do absolutely nothing. However, 99% of its current roles and 99% of its current taxation and spending will disappear. Whether that will take five years or thirty for that first country or group of countries to make the break, is a difficult one to call.

Common Misconception: Do modern economies now demand that you spend more time at work and less at home?

I think this is more likely to be a symptom that people are choosing to find fulfilment in material things because the west is loosing its relationship with God. It is not the problem of the free market but of people's spiritual choices. We might also ask what's wrong with work? People can work hard and still have a good family life. In centuries past people worked far more than we do now. Work is helping other people, leisure is more self indulgent. More work, if it is not at the expense of other things, can be a good thing!

Common Misconception: Does capitalism causes more short term investment than socialism?

You have heard it said that modern capitalism is very short term in its perspective. There are two aspects to this. Firstly, if it is correct to say this then we should bear in mind that the state in general does little investment at all. One of the main reasons for privatisation is that the state owned enterprises have almost always suffered under investment for years. In a service as important as healthcare the British National Health Service built no new hospitals at all in the first 13 years of its existence. Not one. Almost 30 years later there were less hospital beds than when the state took over (Friedman 1979 114) If it had remained private there would have been many more! So government ownership certainly deals with this problem less well than private companies do.
Nothing illustrates the under investment by government better than queuing. Long queues are rare in the private sector because someone else will take the business. In

Rebels Without a Clue?

government they are common. Queues for food on the streets of Moscow; 600,000 people waiting for beds in the British NHS; traffic congestion on state owned roads. None of these things would happen in a privately run investment system.
Secondly, things are changing very quickly today. It may well be sensible to make a decision for a year or three years and then review and change that decision if changing events means that it is not the best thing to provide value for your customers anymore and thus for the rest of society. This so called lack of commitment or loyalty can be in some cases be what creates the most value for us as a society. Rapidly changing to meet our needs is a form of short term decision making, but it is a good thing.

Turner goes into this, explaining that long term relationships work best in an engineering environment where predictability and long runs are important. Reich talks about it in terms of the "stable" inflexible US economy in the 50s and 60s. What we all agree on is that the world has changed, and that in a service orientated, global, Internet world, short term thinking can actually add more value sometimes.
Thirdly, to the extent that short term thinking is a bad thing, it is a personal problem. It would not be remedied by leaving things in government ownership where short termism is likely to be worse. It can only be solved when a society grows in character and faith, something socialism has always deterred.
However, the obsession of the left with high levels of borrowing (admitted by Turner 2001 236) that our children need to pay back in contrast to conservative administration that tend to be more disciplined shows free market ideas tend to encourage a longer time perspective. The exception would be the Reagan administration but that was mostly caused by the increased defence spending that brought down the "evil empire" of socialism which was, of course, a good thing. Of course, in a fully privatised world, governments would not be able to borrow at all and ordinary people would decide their own balance between present and future.
Furthermore, the inflated valuations of Internet companies, irrational though they always were in my opinion and the obsession with "buy and hold", shows an investing public in the US willing to wait a long time for profits and dividends.
The Internet is in any case an equalizing institution. It gives every small individual the ability to reach the whole world. The trends are not towards only a small minority benefiting. In any case socialism is legendary for benefiting a small elite and leaving the rest in poverty. It is capitalism that brings benefits to the masses. Remember in the 19th century industrial revolution that mass production was for the masses.

Short Term Relationships

Another contention is that in the new free market economy business relationships will be short term rather than being based on long terms relationships of trust (Gray 1998 96) That's a distortion. I think trust will be even more important in the new economy than the old. Trust is based on keeping to the agreement. The agreement has changed, no longer is lifetime employment/slowly improving products the agreement.

Rebels Without a Clue?

Now flexible improvement/ rapidly improving products are the deal. Within this new deal particular individuals will make relationships with each other and sacrifice short term gain for long term gain. A freer economy will need more not less trust and good character and the premium on such things will be higher.

Common Misconception: "Are there different forms of capitalism. European, US, Asian which we can choose from?" (Answering Gray 1998 3)

The free market is where government controls none of the economy and taxes are non existent. It would be more accurate to say from these examples then that there are different ways and degrees to which the state interferes with capitalism and limits its effectiveness. The golden egg laying geese of freedom have often been slaughtered by governments. The solution then to all these economies is the same, privatise what has not already been privatised, drop taxes and spending to zero and deregulate unnecessary laws (www.dougieshaw.com/dts1.html under regulation.) That does not mean that in all ways Europe is behind America. Certainly in their labour laws, minimum wages and anti-social insecurity they are further behind than America, but their central banks (and now bank), have been more sensible in not creating booms, they haven't got housing guarantee corporations the same way, their governments military budgets are not as expanded. All countries need to privatise a lot more. The weaknesses of each compared to the others is a function of where one or other is ahead in the race for more market and less government.

There are not different capitalisms for different cultures; there are different degrees in different areas which would do well to converge, not to any Western model, but to 0% tax. When the World Bank report cites the need for good government and an effective state, it is talking about the need for justice, for which we agree but it fails to understand that this functions, necessary as it is can be provided equally well by the market, if the legal context is right.

Democracy as in people voting for say, education policy, rather than getting their taxes back to simply buy what they want is far more culturally relative than the free market. Capitalism and low taxes work everywhere, democratic institutions are neither necessary (Singapore, Uganda, Thailand, 19th century UK) or sufficient (India) for development.

Culture is different everywhere, not all states will be secular. Secularism may well die out. People outside the West still value being in touch with God. That is one of the main ways the rest of the world will diverge with Europe in the coming years.

Gray's assumption is that a country's culture will dictate a different economic system. On the contrary, different people should use the free market tools we talk about in this book to perpetuate their own culture. For example, if their economic culture is to have less inequality they can deal with it themselves using an Internet system that pools funds and distributes it, voluntarily. The state must not do it. Similarly, to preserve heritage we use private property rights traded on markets not the state. Therefore, pure 0% free markets are the best way to express any culture.

Rebels Without a Clue?

The values of the world probably will diversify due to the Internet. It is easier to find common believers across the world, whatever the object of faith. I am not necessarily then looking for a universal civilization anytime soon and when there is one I agree it will probably not be on an Enlightenment model. Personally, I am glad it is not going to converge around Rousseau, Hume and Voltaire! None of this means that we will not converge on one kind of economic system (a pure free market) as the best producer of wealth for everyone, regardless of whether people are Muslims in Algeria or Confucians in China.

Trends come and go, 1970-1985 and 1995 to 2000 the US was the model, in the late 80s it was Japan, in the early 90s Europe. Government created booms and busts usually make and break these favourites. Such fashions should not distract us from the task at hand.

Common Misconception: "Are the prevalence of crises, crashes and meltdowns a problem with capitalism that Keynesianism can solve?

In fact, it rather proves of the effective workings of capitalism. If countries with bad (interventionist) policies are eventually greeted with capital outflows it shows that the system is working to create value for the world by punishing governments that do not get it. Fortunately no one is talking about new "global financial architecture" now as they were in 1997-8. To prevent the Asian or Russian crises the governments should have had floating exchange rates rather than government set ones, free banking with monetary growth illegal, low taxes and less regulation. Then there would have been no crises.
Gray attributes boom and bust cycles to capitalism (Gray 1998 88) despite the existence of a whole genre of literature that clearly demonstrates that its government control of the money supply that does this. Much can be found on this subject at www.mises.org for example. Gray would rather see a Keynesian cycle of government borrowing and spending in bad times to give a bounce to the economy and of paying back in the good times. The trouble is that governments always forgot to pay back in the good times. Keynesianism in practice always means simply running up debt for our future children, mortgaging their future. With its false emphasis on the whole economy without reference to the distorting effects on thousands of situations throughout the land, Keynesianism has been proved worthless long ago.

Like a blast from the past, Gray brings back the ghost of stagflation in resurrecting the idea that you can create a trade-off between inflation and unemployment as if the 70s had not shown us that such Keynesian policies leave us with both high unemployment and high inflation. Connected to this is his comment that global markets leave unemployment without a solution!

Rebels Without a Clue?

The solution to unemployment is abolishing the welfare state, deregulating labour laws and privatising, thus lowering taxes. Such economies all round the world have little in the way of unemployment. He means no solution that does not clash with his socialist dogma.

Even the US which is 30% socialist has virtually no unemployment. Unemployment is a direct and hugely damaging result of socialism in European economies. Therefore, Socialisms effect on the poor is dreadful should be condemned by all that care about them.

In terms of dealing with crises there is no reason why insurance cannot develop for people to cover themselves against these eventualities. Derivatives on these insurance risks can then create incentives for the crisis not to occur. Since most crises are caused by governments to which markets then react, the primary problem is dealing with governments.

For a well explained accessible discussion of the errors of Keynesianism, moral and economic see Hodge (1986).

Bubbles happen whether we have capitalist or socialist policies

America's Stock Market Crash

In one sense I was in a curious position throughout the bubble period of the late 90s because while I agreed with Gilder et al that markets were transforming the world with the use of the Internet, I still did not think Yahoo was good value at 800 times earnings! We were as sceptical as Frank about "Dow 36,000." Our company went short on the Internet revolution with good effect. "The Madness of Crowds" (Frank 2000 105) that Frank talks about was our key text. Financial history is full of such bubbles and they happen in socialist times such as the US 1960s/70s Nifty Fifty Bubble as well as more free market times like 1929 and the present.

That the financiers involved in these booms or at other times, can sometimes be arrogant (Frank 2000 110) does not tell us anything about what kind of system that we should have. Politicians are usually dishonest according to popular belief. Would liberals privatise the government as a result?

It might have been difficult at the time to separate enthusiasm for the free market with belief that the value of the stock market would continue to grow for ever regardless of profits but the two things are quite different. Markets will reflect people's insane beliefs as effectively as their sane ones. The bubble will burst as bubbles always do, but markets are still more efficient than any kind of government process.

The (perfectly) Efficient Market Hypothesis is overplayed

Rebels Without a Clue?

One might think that with all this belief in markets that I am a believer in the investment theory popular in universities knows as the "Efficient Market Hypothesis." This theory holds that all information out is already contained in the market price so only new information can be profited from. It is effectively saying that markets are perfectly efficient. It can be illustrated by the story of the two economists who were walking down the street one day and saw a $100 note. "It cannot be" said one to the other. "If it was then someone would have picked it up"

In the same way markets become more efficient as we act, sometimes we are the ones that pick up the $100 note and bring markets back to reflecting the right price. More fundamentally though, markets are not perfect, they just seem perfect when compared to government processes which are hundreds of times less efficient and more primitive!

Chapter 6

Socialism's killer overheads

Costs of Tax Collection

In order to fund a state run organisation, it is necessary to first pay tax collectors to bring in the revenue. Government bureaucrats then have to administer the revenue and it then has to be administered by the school, hospital or welfare program where "the buck stops". Comparing these huge costs with the costs of simply paying for a service as it is used, reveals the undesirability of the state's programme.
The collection of taxes in Britain costs about £4 billion per year. The administration costs for government programs are about the same. Total savings when these are eliminated (in the latter stages of privatisation), are £400 per household or £132 per person, every year for the rest of the individual's life.
American taxpayers spend $200 billion and 5.4 billion hours working to comply with federal taxes. The IRS employs 114,000 people — twice as many as the CIA and five times that of the FBI. About 60% of American taxpayers have to hire professional tax consultants. The USA loses over $1,000 billion every year from the negative effects of taxation. That translates to $10,000 per household
The world economy is $25 trillion. Through taxation systems, it loses $8 trillion per year. This is immensely wasteful. In a private society this would be extra money in everyone's pockets and more importantly, a real bonus to the most poor. African people cannot afford to pay for services like bureaucracies, regulators and tax collectors, none of whom add significant value to the economy and most of whom detract from everyone's wealth.
Between 1970 and 1995, increased taxation of labour from 28% to 42% in the UK has led to a 4% increase in unemployment. Reducing these taxes to the previous level should solve most of the unemployment in UK, the USA and at least half that in Europe. Abolishing these taxes altogether would entirely banish unemployment. Therefore, socialism-produced unemployment is not exactly good news for the poor!

The avoidance industry

Because taxes are so high, there is an industry of accountants and financial advisers, tax lawyers and bank and insurance company experts who spend their lives helping

Rebels Without a Clue?

people to avoid paying tax. While this industry is of great benefit to people in the current high tax situation, when taxes are reduced to fractions of their current levels, there will no longer be a need for this industry. These people will be released into other more productive projects. This is a particularly large benefit because a significant amount of the world's brainpower is necessarily tied up in these industries at the moment - brainpower, which can be contributing to economic growth in other ways and improving the standard of living for us all. Developing countries with a shortage of skilled labour certainly cannot afford for it to be used in tax avoidance and the pursuit of legal ways around excessive laws and regulations. Decreasing taxation is the only way to stop it being so used.

Taxation is a destructive process

The Free market has won the intellectual debate concerning the most effective and ethical way for society to be run. Fundamentally, the free market is a way for growing wealth, while socialism contains many mechanisms that are fundamentally ways to destroy the wealth of us all. To quote the legal scholar Holmes: "the power to tax is the power to destroy."

How taxation reduces new jobs
To start a small business, the main source of employment for the young poor, entrepreneurs need high levels of disposable income. The ex-managers of larger companies mainly start such small companies. By taxing them heavily, the number of new companies is proportionately reduced. This is especially significant since new companies are usually not funded by banks; which only lend to established companies. Yet, only individuals can be original. Institutions shy away from unconventional ideas, so most of the new companies and concepts have to be funded from the disposable incomes of ex-managers. To tax that, is to take away the opportunities and jobs of the young people they can otherwise employ

Common Misconception: "Would people rather pay tax to make things better?"

People want better education, health, policing, etc. but most people do not understand that these things can simply be privatised and companies can compete to give them better service. Once they understand that is an option they would rather not pay more taxes but pay less and pay for these goods privately. Therefore, it is not that they want to pay more taxes for these things; it is simply that they want these things to be better as they recognize the government is not providing them very well at the moment.
Reich makes this mistake throughout his books and Friedman in an otherwise very good book on globalisation (Freidman 1999 434) has a whole tirade at the end based on this mistake. He thinks it is foolish to just cut taxes and ignore these areas. Of course it is, if you do not privatise them. However, the solution is to get them out of

the public sector where they will never be done well not to waste more money trying to get government to improve them.
Anything that can be made better by paying tax can be made better by the market for half the cost if the correct rights and structures are in place. This includes public transport, roads, parks, the environment, education, health, public safety and everything else. Therefore, Socialists just lack imagination here. See www.dougieshaw.com/dts1.html and www.dougieshaw.com/privatisingeverything.html .

Kenneth Clark was maybe right (Turner 2001 247) that people do not want to go below 40% tax in Britain. However, many of Lady Thatcher's policies were not popular at the time though all including the Turner, Gray and New labour now accept they were necessary and make no attempts to reverse them. The policies that take taxes down to 10% by privatising health, education, policing, justice, defence and so on may not be popular at the time but a few years later everyone will be unable to imagine the government running these entities. When the populace does not understand the issues because the issues are complex or new then visionary leadership against the will of the people is needed for the good of the people. That's what virtually all countries need to bring in the next stage of privatisation.
 If Clark had privatised radically and unpopularly at the beginning of the Tory's last four year term, by the end of it, they would have been popular enough to get back in. We forget that it was his move in the other direction "22 new taxes" that lost the Tories the election. Therefore, sometimes we confuse the views of the press with the voting behaviour of the people!
Additionally, even if it was a good thing to go with the will of the people, Turner himself demonstrates that public spending grows beyond the initial demand of the people for 3 reasons (Turner 2001 266). First, the public sector group that wants more money is much better organized than the public who has to pay for it, Second, governments bribe the electors at election time (with their own money). Third, inertia keeps spending going. These reasons are three more why we should have all activities in the private sector where we know organisations are needed because people use and pay for their services.

Common Misconception: "Do government departments just need more money?"

Government departments always say this. I've never met one that said they were over funded! The point is however that without a change in incentives and structure, more money will not usually solve the problem. It is only when you privatise things so that the owners have an incentive to cut costs and improve service that results happen. Then the sector can get all the cash it wants, from the international capital markets! And they are much better than governments at knowing where the demand is (i.e. where the people need the services most).

Rebels Without a Clue?

Implementation Issues

Why moving to this system helps the government in power.

Moving from one system to another should not be a problem for governments. Austerity programs are unnecessary if the state is privatised. Indeed general prosperity is favourable to the stability of all governments, as are lower taxes. Conversely, raising taxes caused the fall of a host of governments in history. The American War of Independence, for example, was precipitated by imposition of new taxes on the colony by the British government in London. The English civil war was similarly ignited partly by new taxes. Spain lost the Netherlands as a colony through, you guessed it, high taxes. There are also numerous, more recent examples of how increased taxes led to governments losing power. For example, the original George Bush lost power mostly because he promised "read my lips, no new taxes" and yet brought in new taxes nevertheless. The last Tory government in Britain was vulnerable to the New Labour exploitation of the number of taxes they had brought in. On the other hand, governments that had been the most radical in privatisation and cutting taxes namely the Thatcher administrations in the 80s and the New Zealand government led by Sir Roger Douglas were re-elected with huge majorities despite media criticism. Electorates like tax cuts. Here governments can act for the public good and benefit at the same time.

The insight necessary for governments to benefit politically even more greatly from this program is the concept of "twinning".

Tax cuts are good for governments that want to encourage entrepreneurship

After the 1978 tax cuts in the US, the number of new business starts rose form 270,000 to 630,000 per year by 1983 and 5000 new software companies emerged. The capital gains tax cut led to a 14 fold increase in new commitments to venture capital funding from $39 million in 1977 to $570 million in 1978. That's in just a year! By 1981 actual outlays were $1.4 billion!

The further cut in 1981, caused a further surge. The total yearly amount raised in public issues on the stock market rose from $300 million pa in the mid 70s to more than $15 billion in the mid 80s. Therefore, if we want to create investments and entrepreneurship, we know what to do! (Gregorsky 1998 224)

Every year in the 80s the number of software engineers increased by an average of 28% and computer scientists by 43%.

With the Reagan years, the total US asset base has risen from $17 trillion to $40 trillion. (Gregorsky 1998 206)

Twinning

Rebels Without a Clue?

This refers to the theory that tax cuts and benefits should be simultaneous. People will always accept tax cuts. They prefer not to endure spending cuts. They will not appreciate them if they are given separately and will always complain about withdrawals of benefits. This is not the case if the two are done together.

For example, if people are newly going to be directly paying for healthcare, it should be clearly stated that they are getting a tax cut of £2,000 per year to pay for it. Most people will then see the money and they will never, ever vote to reverse it in the future because they will become used to having the extra money resulting from the private system.

If this policy is strictly adhered to, it is a sure vote winner because the party in power is putting money into the voters' pockets and that is the individual's main concern. As individuals spend the new funds, they increase the efficiency of the object (e.g. School or clinic system). While if the government had spent the same funds, the organisation's efficiency would have decreased. The moral is that no tax cut should be awarded without a strongly linked cut in benefits; otherwise an opportunity to improve the economy permanently is wasted. And certainly no benefit should ever take place without a corresponding tax cut to compensate.

An insight from Machiavelli suggests that if leaders do the hard things quickly and all at once, at the beginning of the term; people will forget. They should gradually phase in the popular changes throughout the term. Hard things, in the context of privatisation, refer to those things that are impossible to twin, like controlling the money supply and the possible short-term negative effects of welfare reforms, where there may be a lag between the benefits and the reform.

Austerity/ Structural Adjustment Programs

There is a lot of criticism in the literature of structural adjustment and austerity programs. In some ways these programs are the inevitable results of years of socialist Keynesian excess.

However, I am not in fact in favour of these kinds of programs. A fully orbed privatisation and deregulation program where taxes are reduced 80% over a year or two as education, health, policing ,etc are privatised would provided such a boost to the economy that no austerity would really be created.

Austerity programs are the result of not going far enough. They are politically dangerous and for governments with the courage to do structural adjustment, they would be better advised to follow the advice here. It would be more popular and more effective.

Government Action is involved in the process
While the ultimate goal is to create a society where the sovereignty of ordinary people determines what happens through the preferences they express in their purchases of economic, environmental or social goods, we are not necessarily saying

that the state has no role in the process. In fact to get to the point where this wealth producing phenomena can happen there needs to be dozens of heroic government leaders who are not prepared to settle for socialism but are willing to take strong action in rolling back the state. Japan Singapore, Victorian Britain and Tsarist Russia both developed with strong states. I do not mean this in the sense that state intervention in the economy was good but that they were strong enough to reduce demands for socialism and other growth destroying paths they could have gone down.

So in that sense I am not particularly hostile to Gray's idea that in terms of historical frequency, the regulated economy is a (bad) natural state and free markets need the power of the state to protect their freeness. Of course, it would be private courts that would be used to do this, so an effective legal enforcement system which the market certainly does need does not have to be paid for through taxation.

Chapter 7
Non Economic/ Non Ethical

Common Misconception: Do we need government action to make our families better?

It is charged (Gray 1998 2) that connectedness allows people to separate into physical communities and insurance groups and exclude those with greater needs who would previously have been part of the same community or insurance group. However, these things to the extent that they really will happen were previously reflected in the price people paid for their insurance or house even if it was in the same group as the less well off people. In any case, these prices give people needed incentives to reduce their risks by doing things like stopping smoking or driving carefully. It is not a bad thing to create these incentives either.

Common Misconception: "Did Thatcherism weaken the family"

What weakened the family were 1960s liberal divorce laws and welfare. Gray has completed hypocritically ascribed to limited market reforms what his liberal agenda has produced!
Even fellow anti capitalist Turner disagrees with him: "the rise of single parent families may have far more to do with the breakdown of traditional moral values than with any economic factor" (Turner 2001 243)
In the sense that the free market has equalised women's earnings (they were held down under socialist rigidity) it has weakened incentives of women to rely on men, but he would surely not see an equalling of gender wages as a bad thing!

Common Misconception: Less than the minimum amount to support a family? (Responding to Gray 1998 29)

"The amount needed to support a family" makes it sound like this is a fixed amount. Two hundred years ago, before the free market brought us out of poverty, supporting a family meant feeding and clothing them. It did not mean entertainment, holidays, sweets, a hundred toys per child, etc. It is only the benefits of economic growth that is enabled us to do these things for our families. No one in Britain earns less than the amount needed to feed and clothe a family in the pure sense. Giving people a minimum wage above that, decreases people's incentives to train so they can provide more value to other people and other families. It also stops families' incomes growing as fast. It is in effect an anti family policy. Why should a poor working family pay tax to support a poor family that refuses to work, because that is the real choice

Rebels Without a Clue?

in real life.

Its also not obvious why, if you wanted to redistribute, you should do it through distorting the labour market, which makes people think skills are valuable when they actually are not. If you were going to redistribute, this would not be the best way to do it.

How do we improve family life with systemic changes?

Make alternatives more costly to give incentives for it to stay together: hard divorce, death penalty for adultery, tort damages for sex outside marriage, to give a few more radical suggestions!

Reduce taxes, regulation, etc. to make it easier for people to work less hours.

Publicly declare ourselves Christian nations like Zambia has done so that you ideologically identify with a pro family ideology (in contrast to socialism, for example!)

Privatise education so that the ideology of the schools is pro family rather than pro state. He who pays the piper calls the tune.

Abolish inheritance tax and put more responsibility on the family to pay directly for education, health, etc. in order to make its members depend upon it as a welfare institution rather than the state. That is not to say it won't fail on occasion but the state has also failed in this area. Secondary safety nets can be provided by charity and the church.

Labour mobility

Labour mobility is a problem for families and communities in the sense that grand parents most usually do not move with their children so they loose contact with their grandchildren. US mobile citizens have transitional friendships for the two or three years they live in the one place. On the other hand it means they end up with more friendships in the end this way.

Labour mobility does solve other social problems of course like unemployment. Gray admits (1998 231) that Europe has pools of unemployment mostly because it is not mobile like US labour is!

Victimless crimes are not victimless.

Prostitution, homosexuality and sex outside marriage all attack the family. If as powerful a thing as sex is available in other ways than the family then the institution of the family is inevitably weakened. Having a strong family unit in society aids the prosperity of everyone in such massive and profound ways that the fact that the two people in the transaction consented and that they both gained value from the experience is not enough to outweigh the cost to the security of all the marriages and potential marriages in that society. The problem with prostitution is not the payment. Pro prostitution advocates have argued that there are similar though more subtle exchanges that take place in marriage. The problem is protecting marriage from other sources of sex. Not to say of course that marriage does not have other foundations than sex. Most good marriages, one would hope, have a good deal more reasons for their existence. However, if we reduce the external sources of sex in society then we create unarguably strong incentives for people to work things out.

Rebels Without a Clue?

How to strengthen the family

If we really want to help families we will reduce the role of the state. We will help the future generations by somehow making the division of property in divorce to contain a damage payment to children in the future. If pornographers had to pay for any damage they do by means of rapes, broken marriages, counselling costs etc. then again we might see stronger families.

Common Misconception: Do we need socialism to improve our communities?

How do we improve community life?
Make a faith community the centre of it.
Wall it off; make it more personal, the very thing that Reich does not seem to want. The problem with many of the things that Reich sites is that they are personal problems not system problems. They are things that individuals must take account for, not things that capitalism is responsible for. The nature of the beast is that the system is getting better but the individual in his decisions is getting worse due to the reduction of the historical effects of Christianity in the West.
For centuries people have left their communities in far more fundamental ways than today, travelling to other countries knowing that they would probably never see their communities again. Nowadays, people travelling abroad can email and phone their communities and often watch the TV stations of their home countries in their new ones. Plus there are pros and cons to communities themselves being too close and not as private as we are used to and we are going to experience more of these as the world becomes more information rich.
Reich accepts that the ability to choose your community is a benefit the free market has given us (Reich 2002 196) but somehow thinks that people who add less to society should have the right to live in the same communities as those who add more. This is like saying that someone that decides not to go to college even though they have the ability and instead does an easy job which is not demanding should have the right to drive a new sports car the same as a doctor who has studied for 10 years and works long hours helping people. It is not necessarily justice to have that kind of (voluntary) poor person given some kind of entitlement to live in the same community as people that add a lot of value through the sweat of their brow.
That's not to say that communities will all be as segmented as Reich seems to think. The main reason why rich communities might want to exclude poorer people at the moment is fear of crime. If the changes we suggest in term of privatising courts and policing and some legal changes are effected then that will no longer be an issue. Then communities may well develop heterogeneously, with criminal free low cost housing and high cost housing together in the same area or at least nearby. As Reich points out there are advantages in any case of having those that work for you close to you if you want to find enough of them at reasonable prices!

Rebels Without a Clue?

Schools of course should be private, so the kind of run down, poor school we see under government ownership would probably not exist at all. In general of course, those that add the most value to society will go to better school than those that do not exert themselves so much, but that is a good thing and a great incentive for people to improve what they do for others. There will of course be relatively many poorer people who make the sacrifice to send their children to a better school and some richer people that do not see the value in it, so a mixture will occur naturally. Additionally, schools effectively segment their market by ability to pay by providing "scholarships' which is of course, simply a method of getting more revenue from people that would otherwise not be customers whilst not offending those to whom you are charging more! Again, less segmented that Reich thinks, if crime is dealt with.

The Environment

Government's have a poor record on defending the environment as do regulations. The market is the only institution big enough and powerful enough to defend the environment. Making sure all environmental assets are privately owned and managed competitively and that they are listed and vulnerable to hostile take over by those who think their environmental management is lacking is the only way to protect our important assets.
Where socialism is most consistently applied, the environment is the worst. Therefore, socialist writer John Gray relates "one of the legacies of the Soviet period- a level of pollution unmatched anywhere apart from China." China destroyed all its sparrows, unleashing a plague of insects the sparrows would have eaten. Most of the dams the socialist governments built collapsed creating huge environmental problems. (Gray 1998 149,180) These things do not happen so much, you may have noticed, in capitalist countries. Liberal writers in the west often try to distance themselves from these results of the ideas they profess but they cannot. Entrusting the environment to the government is not a good idea. Private ownership (capitalism) is the best way to protect it.
Gray, an anti capitalist himself, is none the less kind enough to furnish the proof of the environmental hopelessness of his fellow anti capitalists (Smil in China and Feshback and Friendly in Russia)

Common Misconception: Do social objectives and the environment go by the board in free markets?

It's worse than that for socialists. Therefore, socialist objectives are achieved better by markets raising wages through higher productivity growth and creating jobs through freedom and deregulation. Therefore, socialism for all the rhetoric does not actually help the poor. Welfare states keep the poor poor. Labour market regulation far from protecting workers, price them out of a job.

Rebels Without a Clue?

Common Misconception: Are environmental goods inherently collective?

I agree with Turner (2001 278) that environmental costs (like any cost) should be factored in. I believe the environment is important. The myth is however, that this necessarily involves government as Turner implies. Atmosphere issues can be dealt with by atmosphere companies who receive payments for pollution and reimburse any victims of pollution. Local noise rights can be traded on an online market, creating incentives for noise minimization measures. Rivers, lakes, mountains and so on, if owned competitively in such a way their shares can be bought online will lead to the correct trade offs between cheap development of sites of minor environmental value and the much greater expense of development of sites of more importance in a green sense. In other words the market is what would solve the environmental problems of our age, if we would only create markets in these important areas. Turner despite his preference for the European social model at least has the decency to admit in this context that "the market is a tremendously powerful tool which can help us make [these} trade offs in the most cost effective fashion". Whatever the problem: social, economic, environmental, the market is the proven best way to resolve it.
Transport as an environmental issue
Government does not provide as much road surface as people desire. There is no free market so what roads that exist are provided by an irrational government process poor in information rather than an information and incentive rich market one. In a market economy, there would be more roads but not necessarily much less environment.
Road congestion is much greater in cities than in the countryside. In cities population is dense (and I do not just mean the socialists...) and houses are of higher value than elsewhere. It is likely then, in a proper market than the vast quantity of new roads built would be extra layers on the old ones. Making double decker roads (as they do in Tokyo) is about 4 times as expensive as building on the ground but compared to the cost of knocking down houses (per kilometre of houses) it is considerably cheaper. Other options that have been tentatively tried elsewhere but would become common in a world of privatised roads include underground roads and roads that follow the coast in the sea, a few hundred meters from land. Knocking down vast amounts of old houses or destroying trees is not going to be necessary.
Privatising roads with the right to build another road on top being owned by someone else would be an excellent way to create competition in the sector.

Common Misconception: Is it better to replace shareholder rights with "stakeholder rights"?

The idea presented here is that it benefits society to have employees making decisions about what to make in a business on the basis of their own preference particularly about their terms and conditions of employment as opposed to shareholders. However, it is better for society for shareholders to make these calls. The reason is that shareholders only make money if the company makes profits usually. Companies only make profits if they create more value for their customers than their competition, making them strive to constantly improve. Thus things are constantly becoming cheaper and better for everyone in society including employees and less well off people. If on the other hand you let other "stake holders" control the process then they will make the companies work for their own benefit and consumers will not benefit from the same improvements in product and lowering of price. Employees must serve a company and thus consumers. The company serving employees does not help the poor or ordinary members of society.

The question is: what is the source of progress? The source of progress is companies constantly improving to satisfy customers. That's what makes things better. Giving employees the right to interfere with this process can only produce reductions in this process.

So we should welcome investment houses putting pressure on German utilities that had cities represented on its board. (Reich 2002 80) because these kind of distortions are more likely to create value for some customers over others. Similarly, if companies move to cheaper locations: Levi Straus to outside the US, German companies to Asia and South Carolina (BMW), Sweden's Erickson to lower cost London in order to increase profits that should be welcomed. Higher profits can only come from adding value to you and me. It is great if they seek higher profits and it is a great discipline on governments who are living in the past. Its also does far more good to the poor in the third world than any harm it does the selfish socialist workers in the west who will in any case normally be reemployed. (Reich 2002 80, 82)

If profits are high or low, it does not matter, cutting costs and providing better quality with less people is always a process that is necessary to add value to the community. Of course none of this is to say that companies may not find it helpful and beneficial to work as closely as possible with both customers and employees, it is simply to say they should not be legally required to do so.

This is in any case the way the world is going with Germany's equity market capitalization going from 23 to 71% of GDP in the 90s and 32% to 116% in France. (Turner 2001 177)

Owner Manager vs. Shareholder

The difference between stakeholders and shareholders should not be confused with the difference between shareholders being widely spread investors as in the US/UK or owner managers as in Germany (and now Russia). The latter (including family ownership) is as valid as the other way. There is nothing particular about the former. There may well be incentive advantages to workers also being owners. Whichever form of ownership is best for that enterprise should be the one they choose; it is not a matter for government involvement.

Balancing "Economic" objectives against "Social", Environmental or "Distributional" (responding to Turner 2001 45)

Extending the Power of the Market to other areas.

Rebels Without a Clue?

When Turner talks about economic objectives, he means increasing income per person without unemployment. In this sense, we do indeed need balance. However, the last thing we want to do is put a government process in charge of this. This is like using the bluntest tool we have to do open heart surgery. What we want to do is bring the power of the market to each of these areas: creating rights in the environment, privately owned and traded on the market; tax cuts giving power to the family thus strengthening it, and online markets for jobs that ensure an efficient market and full employment provided labour laws are deregulated for the sake of the unemployed. For rights in the environment see www.dougieshaw.com/dts1.html under the heading "The End of Externalities."

Common Misconception: Does advertising create false needs?

The idea that business can make people buy things whenever they want is a delusion that can only be held by academics who have never been in business, particularly a certain Herbert Marcuse of the Frankfurt School of Marxist social theory. If only, say most businessmen, that this was the case! You can persuade people but it is by no means certain that they will buy your message.

Note in this context though, that intangible benefits are not false needs.

When you decide to buy a Coke rather than say, Strike Cola your decision is based partly on taste and partly on the positive associations of youth, fun and excitement that Coke's advertising has led you to associate with Coke. However to have positive ideas recreated in your mind when you drink Coke is an intangible benefit that people have the right to freely choose. It is not a bad thing. People may decide to buy products that you or I might view as inane, stupid, immoral or pointless but the function of the economy is to provide people with what they want. It should be free to do so. To educate and change values is the function of the church and a private value-orientated education system.

Whatever truth remains in the theory of false needs will disappear with the rise of the information age, which will lead to close to perfect information being available about what products are available and their characteristics. Advertising becomes less necessary.

So if advertising is a problem for the socialists; then the market and the Internet once again provide the solution!

109

Rebels Without a Clue?

Common Misconception: Does marketing, journalism and communication inevitably mislead?

There is a thought that media if it has to satisfy the market will produce only what is popular and not what is good (Reich 2002 66). I have some problems with some of what the media produces today but as social phenomena, the argument ignores market segmentation. Market segmentation will provide more quality for a global market and more popular trash for an equally global market.
Months can pass without me watching TV because I regard it from a knowledge point of view as pretty poor. On the other hand I read "The Economist" every week for news and perspective, I read lots of books which are also media and I go to the cinema perhaps on average once every two weeks when what I mostly want is entertainment i.e. a boost in my mood.

The whole point about what's happening at the moment is that media will not play to the lowest common denominator as it has been increasingly doing up till now but different media will play to hundreds of different audiences. Everyone will have what he or she wants to watch.

It could be argued that an opportunity to influence the masses in a higher way has been missed. Now only those who desire "higher culture' will watch it. In the past the ideological basis of the BBC for example, which comes to mind in this context has been statist, which would not have happened if it had been private. Although I personally appreciate much of its cultural output, it would be wrong for me to expect the ,on average, poorer enjoyers of less highly cultured products (e.g. Jerry Springer/ Soap Operas) to subsidise my entertainment. Even if they were richer, it would still be wrong but I suspect in fact, the BBC is a distributor of wealth from poor to rich in providing its cultural product to a relatively small group. Of course, when the appreciation of the good products of a television network is widespread in the population then there is no problem. Good and popular products are being supplied by the market.

There is the question of misleading journalism. This is caused in the US by a legal problem that only makes newspapers liable for intentional libels. Under normal law, one is liable for damage done in negligence as well and this should apply also to media.
I hope that this might lead newspapers who publish stories with big headlines to at least include the main facts or web pages to consult for more information in order that fully accurate stories can be obtained.

Rebels Without a Clue?

The Corporate Governance Problem

Let me say first of all that I think there are real problems with corporate governance in big business and I think it is a systemic problem, and it is a problem with incentives being in the wrong places. However, the problem is much bigger with government where officials have considerably worse incentives to produce what people want, so socialism can only make the problem worse, and regularly does. Nor can regulation help. Regulators do not have the information to make good decisions (ever), nor do they have the right incentives. However, nevertheless it remains a problem that needs to be solved with the right combination of derivatives, markets and technology.

A lot of the compensation problem was caused by a Clinton era law that wages over $1 million would not be tax deductible for the company, leading to a big rise in options packages.
The principle is that people should earn in proportion to the value they create. In 1980s a CEO took home 40 times that of the average worker this rose to 80 times in 1990 and 419 times by 2000 (Reich 2002 75). Now this is fine if the CEO is creating 419 times more value than the average worker is. However, there are problems.

The first is that this was during an artificial boom created by government boosting of the money supply from 1995 onwards. This inflated the price of stocks, property and, one supposes, executive salaries as a results. Therefore, we can see this as a government induced distortion of the market.

The sensible way to set packages would be in my opinion to pay executives in proportion to how much their company moves up in profitability relative to their competitors. Not how much it moves up absolutely, as its easy to be smart in a bull market, and not how much relative to the market in general as different sectors can do well quite independent of the actions of the chief executive. These other factors can be small parts of the package but the main area should be relative out performance of benchmarks.

The other question is long term versus short term. In general, you want to reward actions that increase the value of the company long term such as developing new products, the long term marketing vision of the company, etc. Anyone can increase profits temporarily by firing staff. That is not to say that especially after decades of "corporate socialism" up to 1990 that companies did not need to decrease the prices of their products for everyone by loosing excess staff. Nor to say that these staff did not become more productively employed elsewhere (they usually do.) But it is to say that their needs to be a measure of how the reforms put in place by an executive affected the company 3 years or 5 years after he left. The difficulty of course being dividing the 3 year change from the effect to the new CEO and his changes. While,

111

clearly not easy, this is the kind of package that shareholders need to ensure that new CEOs receive if they want value maximised.

To be fair to executives, their chance of loosing their job, even more than everyone else, is much higher if they do not raise stock price. And again this works to give people incentives to perform at their best and make sure the best people to create value for us are running the companies that create the most value.

Savings and Loans

America's savings and loans bought junk bonds and then famously went bust. This is caused by the fact that the US government publicly insures bank deposits allowing the Savings and Loans to take high risks knowing that the tax payer will bail them out. This is another example of government interference in the economy having huge negative socials effects.

The clash of cultures and military

Gray (1998 100+) argues that the ideology of global capitalism does not necessarily prevent wars caused by removal of strong states that constrained historic tribal rivalries. I am inclined to agree. These things do not fall within the realm of economics or at least not entirely. The interaction between military and economic matters is that the countries with the most efficient, productive economies are the ones that will be the strongest militarily (Kennedy.) Some of these economies will follow the free market, precisely so that they can defeat their historic enemies militarily. That's certainly a bad motive, but it will have the effect of drawing millions out of poverty in the process.

On the other hand, if they have an ideology that is hostile to the West and they associate the free market with the West then they will remain poor and the only way a compassionate world could help them is allow the victims of their more socialist ways to emigrate to the free world. America to its credit has fulfilled this role historically and other nations to a lesser degree.

Gray points out (1998 122) that the Huntington thesis (Huntington) that wars are becoming more between civilisation groups is not entirely true. The Iraq-Iran wars, the Hutu-Tutsi problems in Rwanda and the First World War were all within civilisations. Closer rivalries often exist between similar groups than between widely different one (effectively spoofed in Monty Python's "Life of Brian" with respect to the various "People's Fronts of Judea"))

Behind Gray's analysis is the idea that the free market is "global cultural imperialism" but the free market is a tool. It is not a competing culture. Privatising the maintenance

Rebels Without a Clue?

and revenue production of German castles, Indonesian rain forests, Africa traditional ways of life or whatever is historic that we want to preserve is the most effective way to promote culture. If we want more of this than other people we can get together with other people through online systems soon to emerge in order to privately subsidise it.
Clash of cultures internally
As far as internal conflicts caused by race, religion, national origin and so on the free market is the best solution to these also. Companies valuing ability tend to be far less stratified racially than government organisations. If greater contact between peoples or different groups is the solution then free enterprise will do this better than socialism.

The Threat of Wars

The minimal level of credibility that anti capitalists in general deserve in the current age is lost by Gray in the closing chapter of his book (1998 206+) when without any previous justification he attempts to argue that the coming free market order will lead to more wars.
While I would certainly not argue that economic prosperity (which is what the market does) removes the impulse to war, it is far from clear why it should exaggerate it. Free trade and dependence on other economies does not eliminate the risk of war as 19th century idealists thought it might, but it does reduce it. Wider travel and encounters with other cultures that globalisation increases must surely somewhat reduce the scope of misunderstanding and prejudice. Most importantly, the reduction in the power and resources of the state globally must reduce the potential for their misuse in war. Global free markets will reduce (though not eliminate) the incidence of wars. Rejecting this to promote a dying ideology of government action in not remotely convincing.

"Western Ideologies"

Gray in his discussion of socialism in Russia points out that it was Western, as is he says the Free Market. He says this as if that should somehow disqualify it! Socialism was exported as a Western ideology in the 20th century particularly by Russia itself but also by liberals in the West. It was a dreadful Western invention and should indeed be opposed by all non Westerns and people everywhere. Its roots however are as old as ancient Babylon, Egypt, the Confucian state in China and so on.

The free market may be being exported from the West at the moment but unlike socialism it is a good and right ideology so the fact that it is Western should not be held against it. Additionally, Israel was mostly a free market in antiquity so its roots are not entirely Western and just about every area of the world has in history and

113

recent times got good experiences of the free market to relate. If it works to raise the poor out of poverty, who cares where it originally came from?

Markets and the Psyche

Taylor talked of the factory as being the salvation of man. Therefore, socialist writers claim that now free markets claim that only in the market are people "most fully human; markets are where we show we have a soul. To protest against markets is to surrender one's very personhood." (Franks 2000 xiii) I do not know of any free market writers that actually believe these things but just for the record, none of them are true. Markets have a lot of benefits but creating humans, showing souls and dealing with personhood are not part of it!

Socialism produces ugliness: it fails on artistic grounds. (Dembovsky)

Another problem with the Socialist worldview is that it suppresses freedom of movement and expression. This has produced the bleak, bland and dry eyesore of the Socialist state.

Take Russia for an example. Russia is superior at many arts – like ballet and gymnastics. This is true, but Russians were good at ballet and gymnastics before they were Socialists! Most of Russian art this century has revolved around portraits of Lenin and Stalin. Since 1917 Russia has mostly remained cold, grey and ugly. Even their beautiful architecture is pre-Socialism!

But why do the Socialists prevent freedom of expression? It is because freedom of expression is linked to freedom of thought. As the individual is absorbed and assimilated into the grey mass of the Socialist society, they forget how to think and can be told what to do. The Socialist upper crust must do all it can to ensure that the masses are in a mental coma, so that they can be easily controlled.

Chapter 8

International

Common Misconception: Is globalisation a bad thing?

Globalisation has been accused of hurting workers, undercutting governments, and robbing voters of influence. Analysis shows none of this is true. Technology has far more influence on rich country workers than globalisation (Economist 2001 16).

Common Misconception: "May we sink relative to other countries because of globalisation?"

We may its true, but there is an implied assumption that there is only a limited pot of money that everyone must share (implicitly assumed in Thurow "Head to Head", Goldsmith "The Trap"). In reality whenever trade intensifies and goods are produced cheaper elsewhere, the money that you save from this means you can spend more on other things in your country. It is very possible for all countries to become richer without any others becoming poorer. Every saving from trade creates more money for the world in general.

Common Misconception: Should we protect First World jobs from Third World competition?

The incredible selfishness of first world socialists and trade unionists is dreadful. Third world countries are finally drawing themselves out of dirt and producing products good enough that the West wants them. This is producing new wealth there and lots of new jobs. Therefore, Socialist want to protect their rich world workers at the expense of stopping millions of people coming out of poverty. Here we see the evil of socialism at its most naked! In any case if we save money buying products that are better and cheaper than what we used before, then we have more money to spend in our own economies. Therefore, it does not harm the West in the long run. Some industries may close or move to the developing world but that is all to the good for the people in general.

Common Misconception: are multinationals really a threat to our freedom?

This is the idea that markets or multinationals control the world or that the latter have some sinister purpose. Markets are millions of individuals and companies and all both groups want to do is make money by providing goods and services. The power of the corporation is not a threat to freedom. They only want to buy and sell, this is not a

threat! The nature of corporations is voluntary exchange not force. Political power is the last thing on the mind of the average business executive.
Multinationals account for a third of world output and two thirds of world trade. A quarter of world trade is within the company. Most of them keep two thirds of their assets in their home countries however and sell the same percentage of their products there. (Gray 1998 62)
Gray and other's constantly talk misleadingly of multinationals (or business in general) doing what "they want", "corporate utopias", and "for profits" without any kind of understanding, it seems that what "they want" is to provide us with continually cheaper and better products and services. It is the only way progress happens. Far from being sinister, it is a hugely benign process for the world. Occasional exceptions do not replace that reality.
However Gray at least understands that corporations are as vulnerable to public opinion as governments (Gray 1998 75). I would say more so. Corporations cannot act in defiance of their customers are survive. Governments can and do!

Common Misconception: is it wrong for multinationals to pay workers in the Third world local rates?

Socialist books are full of complaints about wages and conditions of employment in the Third Word (e.g. Reich 2002 18,79.) What they do not seem to understand is that if the multinationals did not employ people in these countries then the people would probably starve. Like any voluntary transaction it benefits both people.
Ok then, they might retort "but they should pay them Western wages". Firstly, these people are not in general as productive as Western workers. If some law was passed to make Western companies pay Third World workers the same as Western workers then Western companies would only employ people in the West to the dreadful detriment of some of the poorest people in the world. That, of course, is what many socialists and trade unionists actually want, and what they are doing to achieve that result under the auspices of compassion is absolutely dreadful. Once again socialist betrays the poor.
The same applies to conditions. If the conditions of labour improve, if they have nicer offices, more light, more wallpaper, less concrete then there is less money to pay wages. Most third workers prefer the wages to conditions. Campaigning for compulsory imposition of better conditions than companies have to provide to attract workers is campaigning for lower take home wages for the same workers. As incomes go up these standards will change when workers start to prefer pleasant conditions to slightly higher wages. That's how it works everywhere. It is economic growth that delivers higher wages and better conditions inevitably if we embrace the market. Trying to create wealth by force never works.
 If companies did choose to be generous and do something beyond the demands of their global customers, what is to say that higher wages would be more compassionate than other forms of generosity. Why would it necessarily be more

generous to pay people more than you need to rather than employ more people than you need to at ordinary wages? In many ways the latter might be the better thing for the country.

Its also worthwhile saying if one company paid their workers more then their products would become uncompetitive. Their products would not provide value for money and you and I would not buy them. Therefore, they do not really have the option to pay their people more as individual companies, at least not in a significant way. The question is whether legislation should force all companies to do so, this would simply put your own national companies at a disadvantage to other nations' companies and they instead of you would prosper and expand in developing nations.

However, as I pointed out above, even if an international agreement could be reached it may well make things worse rather than better for the Africans to pass such legislation.

It is also far from obvious even if one could only buy slightly more expensive products made by corporations that pay their African workers more, that this is the best way to help the latter. Instead of going through big campaigns to try and get corporations to do this, you would be better to buy the cheaper products and send money to Africans directly through charitable organisations. It would probably be a more effective way to do it.

People that talk about child labour in the West have no idea about how things work in the developing economies. In many cases particularly in Asia if you forbid children from doing ordinary things like sewing clothes, then they will starve or become prostitutes. Working there is a far lesser evil than the other things that could happen, particularly to the legions of street children with no parents to protect them. Economic growth will eventually bring everyone to a position where child labour is a thing of the past if we adopt sufficient free market policies but to try and short circuit the normal process could do horrific amounts of harm.

The point is though, that multinational companies normally do pay above the going rate in African countries by the normal market process in order to get the best people and people in Africa generally consider working for them a benefit in terms of their conditions.

Multinationals sometimes do bad things (just like you and I!) like the powdered milk story and the chemical plant in India but these events are very occasional compared to the solid providing of value all round the world that these companies do.

We need to stop criticising them and start celebrating them.

Common Misconception: Will international trade or technology will lead to unemployment?

Even socialists realise this is a myth (Reich 2002 27). People have insatiable wants. If new technology or globalisation causes a process to be able to be done more efficiently which leads to job losses, the money that the company saved may be spent on other workers in other areas. Therefore, no unemployment is created.

Rebels Without a Clue?

In the alternative it could be translated into a drop in price for what they are selling which leads the people saving the money to spend it on other areas of the economy which leads to jobs there.
For the case for Free Trade in more depth see Friedman (1979 40+)

Common Misconception: Is National Competitiveness Theory really wrong?

One of Adair Turner's key themes is that competitiveness makes no sense as it pertains to countries. Companies compete but not countries he tells us.
The examples of people that promote competitiveness theory include Reich, Thurow, Prestowitz (Turner 2001 24). The first two of which have a definite left wing bias.
He is right in reminding us that there is not a limited pot of money for which nations compete. The whole point of trade is that it opens up options to increase the size of the whole pot. However, even assuming the whole pot of investment is increasing, the share of the increasing wealth that a country that is not privatising and deregulating will certainly fall in the future relative to ones that are. More of an opportunity cost than a ordinary cost but a real cost nevertheless.
Similarly, he is right in telling us that these changes do not take place in an exchange rate vacuum (Turner 2001 26) but I do not think this really helps him. Let's look at what happens. A country is determined to stick to socialism so investment leaves and goods and services become more expensive for a given level of quality compared to others in the world (loss of competitiveness) and so people buy them less. If this was Britain where Turner writes from then this would lead to less demand for pounds, which would lead the pound to decline against the dollar, euro, yen etc. other things being equal. This would mean it would take more pounds to buy goods and services from other countries, making British people effectively poorer. Therefore, socialism makes a country poorer in the current globalised age. It is true that the fall in the pound creates a new competitive equilibrium as he points out, but at a new lower level where Britain is adding less to the world and receiving less value in return.
I would mostly agree with Turner that the reason for deregulating labour markets, privatising, cutting taxes, etc. are not solely to do with international trade. They are in my view, due to the inherent superiority of the free market. I would say that these things will help a country's international trade position in a positive way as well as helping its non tradable industries simply as a result of the efficiency improvements from eradicating socialism (government management of anything) in all its forms.
For developing economies however, globalisation is a far more significant opportunity than it is for developing nations. Attracting a small fraction of the global investment available would be nirvana for a small African country. For these countries everything written about international competitiveness is true and then some.
I would further agree with Turner's theme that the major transition to services (especially in-person services like hairdressing, massage, etc) are unaffected by globalisation and that traded goods tend to decline in value with time (to the benefit of

consumers) thus making non-traded goods a higher and higher percentage of incomes. However, not that only applies to manufactured goods. Many services are tradable and will start to be provided over the Internet from poorer countries. This reduces the force of Turner's argument here.

It is further true to say that the ICT trend is more responsible than globalisation in creating inequality (Turner 2001 89)

Common Misconception: can we really cut ourselves off from the rest of the world without cost?

In a word: North Korea.
Ok, its two words.
The Growth of Less Develop Countries is not likely to materially affect the West
I would definitely agree with this point Turner makes. One country turning fully free market in Africa is not going to pose a threat to the industrial base of France or Germany, even if the countries income/head goes up by ten times simply because its economic base is negligible compared to that of the West. Add to this the fact that while traded volumes continue to rise, their prices continue to fall. These add up to good reasons to completely remove EU and US tariffs on African goods.
At continental level both the EU, Japan and the US only do 10-13% of their total GDP with the rest of the world (4-5% with Less Developed Countries for US/EU). At an individual country level however, its 30% (i.e. including also the trade between countries in Europe) (Turner 2001 30)
The danger to any Western country is thus more the effect from any one of their number going more free market. Business already moves from Germany to the US and from Sweden to London because of relatively more free market policies there. Ireland has hugely benefited by being just a little bit more free market. Of course to the country that adopts the sensible, free market policies it is not a danger but an opportunity. Turner does not address this danger/opportunity.
Globalisation and services
Because manufacturing, IT and telephony lend themselves to automation, the prices of these goods become cheaper and cheaper. In face-to-face services like education, healthcare, personal domestic service and restaurants have much slower productivity growth more money is ultimately spent on these. Turner points out that this is a tendency towards localisation. Education and healthcare would of course become much more productive if they were privatised.
This localisation trend has been going on for 100 years, in the sense that shipped manufactured goods because of their cheap price (a product of the free market) are now a much lower percentage of a cities GDP than things like schools, shops, hospitals and sports centres that cannot really be "shipped" anywhere. Trade is increasing now, but this trend is a counter balance to it.

Rebels Without a Clue?

It is true to say that the faster rate of employment growth in the US compared to Europe is in the non-tradable service sector and hence nothing to do with global competitiveness. However, it is got everything to do with having free, competitive labour markets that socialist Europe has not cared for their poor enough to implement, as if welfare will replace the self-respect and dignity of work. However, we need to concede that US employment growth is not really much to do with globalisation.
Globalisation Déjà vu
We have indeed been here before. Before the First World War, borders were relatively open. No one needed passports. Britain's trade intensity (international trade as a percentage of GDP) was 26% in 1910, and is 29% now. (Turner 2001 31)
In the post war, world output has grown five fold and trade 12 fold.
Capital Controls, the Tobin Tax and accurate pricing

To put control on capital in today's world (Hines 200 93) or to tax it as it comes in is to say to the international community that you do not want investment. It has plenty other places it can go. I personally would be reluctant to invest in Asia again after one of my clients had their money trapped there by capital controls after the Asian crisis. These policies are a form of theft, and no one in the new economy wants to be stolen from.
Furthermore, currency is a form of pricing, to fix or "manage" currencies is to pretend they are worth more or less, than they are. This leads to distortions in supply and demand that lead factories to be build in anticipation of needs that do not materialise when the currency stops being manipulated by government. As the Soros/Bank of England incident showed, this can be very expensive for governments (and thus taxpayers) to do in any case.
DeRosa (2001) in "In Defence of Free Capital Markets" powerfully refutes the case for capital controls for those who want further reading on this subject. He shows in this book that practically all the crises of the 90s were caused by having non-floating exchange rate regimes. That is to say, they had fixed or "managed" exchange rates. Government interference was as always the problem and not the solution.
He further shows that contagion usually does not strongly affect nations with free market policies and thus that crises are usually just discipline on socialist leaning regimes. Proof that the market is working properly not that it has any problems needing fixed.
"Localisation"
If one wants to understand why globalisation is, benefit minus cost, a good thing, you need look no further than Colin Hines book "Localization". Here he argues, I kid you not, that business should be forced to produce in a country if they want to sell there! This means that instead of having 20 factories in China with huge benefit to the poor people there, a small toy seller would have to have one in each of the 250 plus countries of the world. If labour was a major component of the price of the goods then that would raise the price of toys in the West by a factor of perhaps as much as 30

Rebels Without a Clue?

times. (This is working on a $1000 per month minimum wage in Britain and a $30 per month wage in China.) A five-pound doll would now be a hundred and fifty. Of course, all these workers in developing countries would also be out of a job. And he would like to do this to virtually every good on the planet (Hines 2000 68)

He says quite plainly (Hines 2000 257) he does not believe in comparative advantage (this is Economics 101!) which explains why the French make wine and get bananas from Uganda (or wherever) even if they can also make bananas better than Uganda (with capital). The key fact is that the French are better at making wine by a larger margin than they are better at making bananas. Some countries are better at making some goods than others. They may also have a comparative advantage in different areas. Hines wants to neutralise this and have everything produced everywhere by force of law! Even if the price rises in our Chinese example do not apply across the board, doing this with every good in the world could raise prices by 10 -20 times and thus reduce the income of the West to 5% of its current level. What a wonderful idea! Not.

Realising that globalisation is doing the opposite of what Hines proposes helps us understand the good that it is doing!

The other insane things about Hine's policies to "stop Trans National Companies from relocating or threatening to relocate" is that with these kind of polices none of the TNCs would locate there in the first place. They certainly would not be inclined to invest in African countries with small markets. Hines policies would ruin Africa if anyone believed him and this is particularly scary since I bought his book in Kenya, which means it is available there.

Voluntary Localisation

I am not against things being produced for a local market if that is the most efficient way to do things. If markets are left free some goods and significantly, most services will be produced locally. That is fine. What is wrong is forcing things into ways that are not what people want (which is another way of saying what the market demands.) Community action initiative, local mutual organisations and co operatives if they work better (unprotected) than limited liability corporations at supplying needs then more power to them (Hines 2000 47). However, if they need tax payers money to survive (as Hines thinks they do (Hines 2000 57) then rather let the need be supplied by a company. It is simply a waste of tax money which if reduced would probably be creating extra jobs to subsidise a way of meeting needs which is less effective than other available ways.

Hines recognises (2000 245) that the protectionism measures he recommends are the same ones that have failed since the 1930s. He basically argues the same "this time it will be different" argument that every protectionist regime has always argued. He recognises that the powerful used it as a way of controlling their markets without improving things for others. He does not explain what will stop them doing this again. (Friedman in "The Lexus and the Olive Tree" gives examples on what has happened with this dangerous kind of policy recently on p229-230)

Rebels Without a Clue?

Anti Globalisation policies would not in reality do anything its advocate's claim. (Hines 2000 256) It would not create jobs as it leads to structural rigidities in the labour market a la Europe. It would not improve the environment, as people in the West would not be able to buy up environmental assets in Africa and elsewhere to compensate their people for keeping them pristine. It would not ensure the provision of basic needs or reduce poverty or even inequality necessarily as it would slow economic growth reducing income growth, it may also allow local elites to centralise power with monopolies free from international competition. One can best increase community cohesion by other methods explained in the appropriate section..

Chapter 9

Insecurity

We have met the enemy and it is us
It is a theme of Reich's book and it is definitely true. If we want to enjoy "The age of the terrific deal" then we need to understand that the other side of these deals is flexible working hours, insecurity of employment and so on. One cannot exist without the other.

Can government cushions people against insecurity? Reich's shaky solutions.

Earnings insurance is not a bad thing, but the idea that it should be provided by the government is a dreadful one. Government does not have the incentives, information or ability to segment to do this. It would be a mammoth waste of resources, especially since many would not want to participate and should not be forced to.
Security and Options
Options can give you all the security of lifetime employment at a price, if you want to pay it. However, do not impose it on the rest of us!

Common Misconception: Is capitalism a casino?

Those who do not understand stock markets who look at constantly changing prices liken it to a casino. For people who buy or sell shares without understanding it certainly is a gamble. However, stock markets are not intrinsically a gamble like the turn of a roulette wheel.
Stock markets are initially a way for companies to raise money and then the secondary markets provides a market for management as bad managements can be more cheaply replaced through takeovers if their actions cause the share price to fall. For investors who understand the markets, they provide a way for even small investors to benefit from the returns companies provide by serving consumers to the best of their ability.
They look more like casinos during booms where governments have created artificial money supply increases by manipulating interest rates. The solution, of course, to these manipulations is to ensure it is constitutionally impossible to increase or decrease the money supply (see www.dougieshaw.com/dts1.html under The End of Inflation)

Rebels Without a Clue?

The Switchover to a Value Creating Economy (Reich 2002 72-74)

Mid century, executives were a lot more relaxed in the value destroying stability that prevailed at that time. "Men went about their work with no particular sense of urgency" this stability enabled the head of Standard Oil to talk about "balancing the interests of all interested groups: shareholders, employers, customers and the public at large." If this sounds fine to you, consider if someone was looking after your house while you were on holiday and decided to use it for the benefit of "yourself, your employees, your customers and the public at large!" This is the stakeholder mentality, which is tantamount to theft and does not create as much value as it distorts incentives. Employees if they are seen to "own" the enterprise like shareholders will not produce the same way as if the goal is clearly seen as maximising profits by pleasing customers.

Executives at that time had fairly relaxed lives, "entertaining lavishly...pursued several rounds of golf per week, engaged in highly visible acts of charity .dabbled in public affairs". Nowadays, on the other hand, they "view their sole duty as maximising the value of shareholder's [owners] shares ...by cutting costs and adding value". Once you understand economics and you realise that this means products that are rapidly increasing in value and decreasing in price you realise how much better the new way is to the old. In addition, as I never miss an opportunity to point out, products getting cheaper faster is the main way the poor come out of poverty, which capitalism does far better than socialism despite its lies to the contrary.

So when you here about a "singular focus on earnings" think "good thing for the community!"

Various things created the changeover. One turning point was the first hostile takeover in the US in 1974 when International Nickel bought Electric Storage Battery and sacked the whole board. In the remainder of the 70s there was another 12 hostile takeovers and then in the 80s, there were 150. Socialists who complain about fat cats should applaud this kind of thing (as do I); because it means those who are being paid a lot of money and not producing value for "the people" loose their jobs. Surely, this is better than a protected elite? This created an economy where unions were pressed from their selfish behaviour that raised the prices of goods for the poor, cheaper supplier prices were found and factories were moved elsewhere in the world (to the great benefit of many needy people in the rest of the world who have left poverty behind them now.)

For a shocking story of how unions destroyed British prosperity in the 20th century see Chapter 3 of historian Paul Johnson's "Wake up Britain" (1994). He related that after the late 40s "the unions began to inflict critical damage on the British economy." In fact, he relates, while in the next 20 years GDP in Europe multiplied by five, the British economy only doubled. Union power moved international port traffic from London to Rotterdam. Unions imposed thousands of "ghost workers' on newspapers causing many to close down. They destroyed the car industry, once the second largest in the world. One of its CEOs had to attend 365 union meetings one year, which tells us about the degree to which management was unable to run a proper business. When socialists complain about the departure of manufacturing from Britain they conveniently forget that it was their socialist friends that caused it.

"People are scared of loosing their jobs due to rapid change"

While this may be true, the solution is not to be socialist; rather we must lower taxes and abolish minimum wages, social security and trade union immunities in order that we can have full employment in a free market. The solutions socialists use for these problems are the very things that cause them.
In a pure free market it is always very easy to get jobs as socialist restraints on the labour market clearing are gone. This in itself reduces the "middle class insecurity" talked about by Gray (1998 108). Internet labour markets and derivatives contracts on job security can allow people to trade income for security without the need for any kind of socialism.
"If positive change is more rapid, life is less predictable." That's true, but in a free market society where businesses have to produce positive benefits to survive, the fact that new benefits are coming in an unpredictable manner is hardly a bad thing. If you have to change jobs more often, if the economy is growing faster then it is more likely than before to be to a better job. Again, this is hardly a bad thing. If people prefer predictability there will still be predictable job, but at a lower wage, buts there's still a choice.
The difference, so far anyway, in job security, is not that high. The average amount of time in a job has fallen from 5.8 years in 1970s Britain to 4.9 in the mid 90s.
Increasing security for some decreases security for the rest.
People that hark back to an era of greater security forget that it was unequally divided. Unions created great security for their members, but that reduced security for people that now had to deal with products that were unpredictable in quality because firms had no ability to sack bad employees. Protecting industries from price signals created insecurity for those that had to compete with subsidised industries. For more on this subject see Hayek (1944 89+).

Common Misconception: when companies fail, does that mean the market has failed?

On the contrary, companies going bankrupt are proof the market is working! When unethical companies go under and their directors change, that is proof that the market along with law effectively deals with the bad guys.

Rebels Without a Clue?

Similarly, Barings Bank's failure was a result of their lack of systems, and their problems provided incentives for other companies to tighten up. It is not a problem with the system when individual companies fail.

Chapter 10

Individual Situations and Countries

Europe

Socialists sometimes defend Europe's abysmal "social" model by saying that Europe's productivity is higher than the US. However, this is only because the US has more people working. When France divides its output by its workers of course, it is going to be higher when the denominator is missing 10% of the workforce!
The Euro zone runs a surplus and the US a deficit on the current account. This means the US imports lots more goods than it exports, and Europe the other way round. However, to do that means that the US must fund that on the capital account by receiving lots of funds inwards in investment and that Europe on the other hand is investing a lot more out of the area than is being invested into it. This is hardly a necessarily healthy situation for the long run.

Given the recent Clinton manipulation of the money supply creating an artificial boom, I do not think the US situation is sustainable, but that does not mean the European situation is too hot either! Europe will resist the full application of the free market tooth and nail which is a major opportunity for developing countries in Africa and elsewhere to rapidly move to fully privatised states and capture European production. Even one percent of European production could bring any African nation substantially out of poverty and Aid dependence.
For measurement issues related to US vs. Europe prosperity and productivity comparisons see the appropriate section.

US productivity is also partly higher because of a few other factors according to Turner (2001 156). It has lower population density on average, which makes land cheaper and thus roads less congested and retail stores larger and more efficient. It also has common language and laws making for larger companies, long production runs and more economies of scale. It also may turn out that the technology promoted growth of recent times will be experienced in Europe also as it adopts the new Internet technologies in a more complete way.

In no sense is continental Europe traditionally anti free market. In the decades after WW2, it had a far smaller state than it has now, and grew proportionately faster (EU15 grew 4% between 1950 and 1973). It simply has to return to that older tradition. It was Britain in the 70s that was the sick man of Europe because of its socialist policies. It is only since the 80s Britain has become less socialist than the rest of Europe. Nor is the US perfectly free market now, its growth would be much higher if it was. Its productivity growth slowed down dramatically (to 0.8% pa) between 1973 and 1996 because of its more regulative and higher tax policies.

Russia

Russia is often used as an example of the market operating without government. It was not. First, it was an example of socialism collapsing, as it always inevitably will after a century or so because it is inherently parasitical. The move towards capitalism involved the collapse of existing institutions because they had been collapsing for years. It is not the fault of the capitalist system that it makes clear the collapse of 70 years of destructive socialist policies. Other countries that do not start socialist do not encounter these problems becoming more free market. Gray even accepts this himself at least to some degree. Indeed, he points out that it did work to some degree in Poland and Bolivia, economies that had not to the same degree been destroyed by liberal/ socialist policies (Gray 1998 142-3).

Furthermore, the chaos that happened in Russia was the result of the government not privatising the justice and policing system to provide law and order in an effective manner. Yet they were also guilty of not providing it themselves as a government. The rule of law is essential for prosperity but the state will never provide courts and police like the free markets can. Therefore, its problems are insufficient free market, not insufficient socialism. There is no doubt there are far more goods and better goods in the shops of those countries that have left communism behind. Nor is their any doubt that their welfare system was collapsing whether they had turned to capitalism or not.

The crime, the mafia and the corruption existed during the Soviet regime. Indeed in a communist state, it is the only way anything can function at all (Gray 1998 155). The point is only that this continued as the economy was normalised not that the shock therapy created it. The mafia are estimated to earn 40% of Russian GDP and provide a similar percentage of start up capital for businesses. Most businesses pay 10-20% of their revenue to mafia groups who then protect them. Given this state of affairs and the near impossibility of defeating around 150 mafia organisations, a feasible solution would be to legitimise these organisations as private police and allow them to make money from enforcing the law rather than breaking it.

Like the French Revolution, the Russian revolution was a case of "out of the frying pan into the fire." The situation beforehand was not ideal in either case. Feudalism like Socialism is inferior to the free market. However, it was nothing in terms of repression to what came after. The Tsar's secret police had 161 full time employees

Rebels Without a Clue?

supported by 10,000 soldiers. By 1921, the secret police was 250,000 people not counting the army.

In 1992, price controls were lifted on 90% of goods in the shops, causing vanishing queues and price rises of up to 250%. Wages only rose 50% and companies became extremely profitable for a little while. Living standards initially dropped about 50% and people kept themselves alive by growing their own food. State services have deteriorated (as a result of them not being privatised). Many people are poor, but this is of course, more the result of 70 years of socialism than anything in the last few years. Therefore, Socialists have the audacity to blame the adjustment program for the poverty their own policies have created over decades. Inequality is not particularly a problem being less than the US, closer to the UK. The problem is poverty, which comes from insufficient economic growth over decades. If there had been no adjustment program, the state would still have collapsed and people would still have been poor.

The fall in GDP was mostly a *recognition* of lower value more than a drop. Nothing provided without a market can be measured. Eastern Block economies exaggerated their production and what it was worth in monetary terms. When they switched to a real economy, they discovered through the price mechanism what they were producing was worth a lot less than they had thought. That which was real was mostly due to the drop off in military orders. Russia's GDP was 30% military! Within six months of the Soviet collapse, orders were down 40%. This happened before the shock therapy.

In some ways, there are lessons to be learned. The proceeds of the privatisation could have been better directed across the whole economy if the drops in living standards had been anticipated. It might have been better to do things more gradually to allow businesses and individual's time to adjust. This would be feasible in places where there is no anti capitalist opposition. The problem created by the very people that complain about "shock therapy" is that if you do not do the right things quickly while there is a consensus then they may never be done.
Gray's contention that free markets will not work in the Russian scenario is nevertheless false. His blind spot is he does not understand that the free market can provide education, policing, justice, etc. and indeed provide them better. The free market, fully applied, is thus the solution to Russia's problems as everywhere else

Mexico

John Gray's shameless discussion of the Mexican crash briefly alludes to the fact that Mexico, for a long time an extremely socialist country, was a result one of the world's most unequal ones. For all his opposition to temporary inequality with benefits long term, he fails to repent of policies that created much worse inequality in places like Mexico without the corresponding economic prosperity for the majority that everyone agrees the market brings. Government intervention in the currency and banking sectors of the economy, like most financial crises, created the Mexican crises.

The implication that free market reforms are not good for all the people is simply wrong. Picking a particular year is not a statistically valid line of argument. It is well established now that high economic growth for a country is correlated with high economic growth for the poor (e.g. World Bank) and no one who considers the twentieth century could really argue that socialism creates more economic growth. Far from it.

Germany

The idea that German's social model is in some substantial way better than a more free market model is false. The lack of cost cutting makes products more expensive for everyone who buys them, especially the poor. Accommodating stakeholders cause consumer needs to be met less well as companies start acting for their own good (employees) rather than those of others (consumers). One of the main reasons why German costs of labour are so high are taxes to fund government departments. Privatising education, health, etc. so they operate as corporations on the German model and reduce taxes by 80% would delay for a long time the need to make German markets more flexible in order to stop companies moving abroad. Privatising these things in fact lowers labour costs far more than any flexibility enhancing measure ever could.

The US, crime and race

According to the socialists, America is the source of all evil and a complete promoter of the free market. The American people would love for it to be true. Sadly, the various levels of US government still take more than 30% of the GDP of the country. It also still has a long way to go. According to Gray (1998 217) the free market is an American project. This is mostly nonsense. The fact that the World Bank/ IMF promote the free market these days is a result of a new global consensus based on the fact that government action (socialism) has proved ineffective. These organisations may be based in the US but countries all over the world are following more and more free market policies. They are not necessarily doing this on a "Western model" as Gray is keen to point out. However, in not adopting that model they are often going further towards a complete free market than "the West" is, and rightly so. For example, China has privatised roads and floated them on its stock markets while the West still plays about with government-orientated programs like

Rebels Without a Clue?

Build, Operate, Transfer and Public/Private partnerships. Health is further along the path to privatisation in most developing countries than in Europe. I personally find the African governments I talk to far more open to further privatisation than those in the West. Therefore, it is true, often the non-West is leading in the privatisation process, and a good thing too!

Gray also would like to ascribe any problems that are higher in America to its more free market structure but usually the evidence points against him.

He goes as far as to say of America "Families are weaker in America than in any other country" (Gray 1998 2). Really? Than Sweden, erstwhile jewel in the socialist crown? Some more serious study would be good here! For example, America has historically had higher crime than Europe however, Britain has now caught up with the US in many categories and the rest of Europe is not far behind in catching up. On the other hand, many countries with much lower ratios of tax to GNP have much lower crime such as Hong Kong, Singapore, Thailand. This suggests the causality for high and low crime rates might rather be found elsewhere. The number of police officers per capita is inversely correlated with the crime rate suggesting a private policing environment where more companies can enter the policing market to reduce crime. Secondly, the higher the cost of crime in terms of penalties, the less of it occurs, so lax penalties may also be to blame in countries that suffer from high crime (including South Africa.) A fuller discussion of these issues can be found at www.dougieshaw.com/dts1.html or in one of my previous books "Privatisation for Prosperity" when describing the privatisation of Justice and Policing.

In terms of racism, in one area, socialism definitely perpetuates rather than reduces racism and that is racism in hiring. In competitive markets such as IT and advertising, there are usually much more representative racial and gender groups than in government. The reason is that free market competitive areas cannot afford not to hire talent. It is their most important asset. Prejudices cost money. In contrast, when you are a government department you are spending someone else's money, which is why there is much more prejudicial hiring, and the accompanying lawsuits in this sector. Privatisation will lead to more merit and less racism.

The Asian Crisis

Government action in the form of fixing currencies caused these crises. Since these economies are otherwise fairly free market the negative effects were soon reversed. Yet, despite these problems, due to their lower tax rates and less socialist policies, their economies soon bounced back to at least double the economic growth rates of more socialist countries once again. Gray was wrong in forecasting a long-term depression for these countries (Gray 1998 219) precisely because he does not understand how effective market orientated economies are at adjusting to crisis quickly.

IN the year to 4th quarter 99 Korea grew a massive 13% and Malaysia 11%. Turner however, despite realising that more socialist policies slowed growth in Latin America, sees their growth as wholly catch-up rather than a long term effect of lower tax to GDP ratios i.e. a more privatised economy. Now that many of the Asian economies have caught up with the West (especially in PPP terms) and have not slowed down to 1-3% it is difficult to see how we cannot attribute the continued growth to the far lower levels of state spending. Empirical analysis between low total tax take and economic growth bears this out. Catch up can only go so far as an explanation.

Japan

If as Gray suggests (Gray 1998 227+) the Western consensus is that Japan should "cut taxes, expand public works and run large budget deficits" then I would disagree with them as much as Gray. Rather it should cut taxes in conjunction with cutting spending as the major services still (badly) run by governments are privatised. Deregulation would also wake up the economy. Japan's main problem is that unlike the rest of Asian in the 1997 crisis, its institutions do not allow it to take a sharp adjustment which allows assets that were bubble priced to be accurately priced and for everyone to proceed on a more accurate basis.
Not inflating the economy in the first place of course, would have been a better strategy for Japan. As with the US 1930s depression, the government should have done "nothing, sooner" to quote the great economist Ludwig von Mises.
Gray alleges that deregulating the labour market will create unemployment like Western countries and that the Japanese do not have a welfare state. This misunderstands that the West has unemployment *because* it has a welfare state! If there is no welfare state then wages just go down for a while, everyone is re employed at a lower price and the extra value goes into the economy as lower prices for goods or higher wages again after the market has recovered. It is the labour market restrictions favoured by the likes of Gray that stop this beneficial process taking place! We should not forget that the full employment policies pursued by Japan up till now are an artificial full employment where people unproductive in a particular role are nevertheless kept on. If they had been a bit more "ruthless" as Gray puts it then the fired people would have been re employed in other more productive processes needing to faster economic growth for the poor and everyone else than what actually resulted.
In this section, he talks of redefining economic growth in terms of "goods, services and lifestyle." I do not know when the last time was he studied the components of economic growth but that is what they already contain. If people buy insurance

Rebels Without a Clue?

policies or futures contracts to reduce the insecurity of economic life in the new economy then they will come up in economic growth stats, rest assured.

The Market and Democracy

Gray argues that the market and democracy are rivals not allies. I agree. The order of the future is the market (where we each decide what school, hospital, roads etc. we want to use) as opposed to democracy (where we vote for people who will supply us with these things in a form that may or may not be what we want.)

Common Misconception: What creates a dependency culture?

Gray's argument turns from the sublime to the ridiculous where he actually argues that free market reforms create a dependency culture because privatising council houses somehow led to higher levels of housing benefit. If there was no housing benefit, and people stayed where they could afford, then the dependency culture would not be created. Everyone would be working.

Crime

Gray constantly comments that in Britain in the 80s and 90s crime continued to grow. Crime control was one of the areas left in the realm of that state. That is why it continued to grow! If it had been privatised too in the way I suggest in "Privatisation for Prosperity" then crime control would have become as effective as the rest of the economy was becoming.

References:

Modern Anti Capitalists aka the rebels without a clue …..are indicated RWAC

Anderson, William L."Sweden: Poorer than you think" (posted May 16 2002 www.mises.org) edited by Colin Dembovsky)
Abrahams, Jay 2000 "How to get everything you can from all you have"
Barro, Robert J. 1997 *Getting it Right: Markets and Choices in a Free Society* (Cambridge: MIT Press)
Bonnor, Bill 2002 The Daily Reckoning a daily Newsletter on finance and economics, freely available from www.dailyreckoning.com (Bonnor introduced me to the phrase "Rebels Without a Clue")
De Rosa, David F. 2001 In Defence of Free Capital Markets (NJ: Bloomberg Press)
De Soto, Hernando 2000 The Mystery of Capital. (London: Bantam Books)
Dembovsky, Colin 2002 writing on www.dougieshaw.com
Economist World in Figures
Economist Aug 23 97
Economist 2001 Globalisation (London: Profile Books)
Feshback, Murray and Friendly, Alfred 1992 Ecocide in the USSR (London: Aurum)
Frank, Thomas 2000 One Market Under God (London: Vintage).
Friedman, D. 2000 Law's Order. (NJ: Princeton University Press)
Friedman, M. & R. 1980 Free to Choose (Orlando: Harcourt Brace)
Friedman, Thomas 1999 Lexus and Olive Tree. (London: Harper Collins)
Gray, John 1998 False Dawn: The Delusions of Global Capitalism (London: Granta) RWAC
Gilder, George 1981 Wealth and Poverty (New York: Basic Books)
Gilder, George 1984 Spirit of Enterprise (New York: Basic Books)
Gregorsky, Frank 1998 Speaking of George Gilder (Washington: Discovery Institute Press)
Hayek, F.A. 1944 The Road to Serfdom (London: Routledge)

Rebels Without a Clue?

Herrnstein, Richard J. & Murray, Charles 1994 The Bell Curve (New York: Free Press)
Hines, Colin 2000 Localization: A Global Manifesto (London: Earthscan) (RWAC deluxe)
Hodge, Ian 1986 Baptized Inflation. (Tyler, TX: ICE)
Johnson, Paul 1994 Wake up Britain. (London: Orion)
Kennedy Preparing for the Twenty first century
Keirsey, David. 1998 Please Understand Me 2(Del Mar, CA: Prometheus Nemesis)
North, Gary 1989 Marx's Religion of Revolution Fort Worth. ICE (all of Gary North's books are downloadable at www.freebooks.com. Few writers are as interesting and informative. You can also get his free newsletter from the same place.)
Rand, Ayn 1957 Atlas Shrugged (New York : Penguin)
Rand, Ayn 1936 We the Living (New York: Penguin)
Rand, Ayn 1946 Capitalism the Unknown Ideal (New York : Penguin)
Reich, Robert 1997 Locked in the Cabinet (New York: Knopf) RWAC
Reich, Robert 2002 The Future of Success (London: Vintage) RWAC
Reich, Robert 1991 The Work of Nations (NY: Alfred Knopf) RWAC
Reisman,George Some Fundamental Insights Into the Benevolent Nature of Capitalism www.mises.org October 25, 2002 (George Reisman is professor of economics at Pepperdine University's Graziadio School of Business & Management in Los Angeles, and is the author of *Capitalism: A Treatise on Economics* (Ottawa, Illinois: Jameson Books, 1996). His book is available through Mises.org or Amazon.com. His web site is www.capitalism.net.)
Rothbard, Murray 1970 Power and Market (Kansas City: Universal Press Syndicate)
Russel, Robert A. Winning the Future (New York: Carroll and Graf Publishers 1986)
Shaw, Douglas 2002 Privatisation for Prosperity (Johannesburg: Global Press)
Shaw, Douglas 2003 www.dougieshaw.com The analysis mentioned analyses the 66 of countries of the world, eliminates 18 with inflation over 50% pa (as any effect on growth will be masked by the inflation effects.) The top 24 and the bottom 24 countries are then analysed using simple averages. It is especially telling that these statistical results are this clear without needing to control for other variables or use more sophisticated techniques. Spreadsheet available at the website.
Smil, Vaclav 1983 The Bad Earth: Environmental Degradation In China London: Zed Press
Turner, Adair 2001 Just Capital: The Liberal Economy (London: Macmillan) (Formerly Director General of Confederation of British Industry) RWAC
World Bank: 1990 Adjustment in Africa
World Bank 1997 World Development Report 1997 *"The State in a Changing World* (New York: Published for the World Bank by Oxford University Press, 1997) * World Bank is in Washington*

Rebels Without a Clue?

Further Reading and Action

You can get further information on subjects in this book at www.dougieshaw.com.

This website will also provide information about getting involved in setting up fully private countries in the future and in buying privatisation stock issues throughout the world.

You can get involved in private policing and bringing down crime in your country at www.againstcrime.com

You can reach the author at dougieshaw@bigfoot.com

He has also written:

"Privatisation for Prosperity" where he explains practically and in detail, how to privatise the areas of education, health, policing, justice, roads, the environment, inflation control and many other areas. He also gives examples of where its working elsewhere in the world.

"A Question of Freedom": a novel set in a country, Libertonia, that seceded from Tanzania in 2007 and became the world's first completely tax free state where everything is privatised. The president of the EU creates trouble because he is unhappy with the amount of business going to this upstart African state. Then Zimbabwe invades. Its not so full of war and action however, that there is not time for the intrepid CEO of Libertonia to fall in love and for these relationship issues to be explored in full. Something for everyone.

Released July 2004

"Global Citizen": A humorous and informative tale of the authors travels in 30 countries.